When the Thousand Years Expire

When the Thousand Years Expire

John Class

Aventine Press

Published by Aventine Press
1023 4th Ave #204
San Diego CA, 92101
www.aventinepress.com

ISBN: 1-59330-460-9

Library of Congress Control Number: 2007922277
Library of Congress Cataloging-in-Publication Data
When The Thousand Years Expire

Printed in the United States of America

Prelude

We have traced human history from Armageddon through World War II. Then we traveled through the Dark Ages of repression and cruelty—all the way to the very beginning with our first parents, Adam and Eve. Lev Aron and his former wife, Rebekah, have been our guides as we looked through various windows during the regeneration. Each period of time brought vivid reminders of evil expressing itself in many forms of behavior. Sometimes civil and religious forces worked closely together in the repression of mankind.

We visited former despots like Diocletian and Nero, and we found that evil came from either stern discipline or from a lack thereof. The heroes of history have been the builders and the planters, the caregivers and nurturers, those who struggled for better conditions. Now they are rewarded beyond their fondest dreams, receiving abundant refreshment in the regeneration.

As the thousand years of Christ's reign draw to a close, an urgent new dilemma comes into view. All people are not alike. Yes, they all learned to conduct themselves appropriately and to keep within the limits of righteousness. Yet, the Lord must separate the "sheep" from the "goats" (Matthew 25:31-46). This test is the focus of our final book of the regeneration series. Those who have lived for hundreds of years cannot believe that their lives are not ensured because of God's love. The "goats" are completely surprised at the judgment raised against them, just as the "sheep" seem unconscious of their own goodness and generosity.

It is not until the thousand years of Christ's reign are ended that the final test is placed upon men. When Adam and Eve were in Eden they did not have eternal life, but were on trial for it when the great tempter Satan set out to deceive them. They failed the test and were condemned to death. When the thousand years are ended, Adam and Eve and all their redeemed children will individually stand trial for everlasting life. This time they will be wiser and more experienced knowing what sin and death are like, because they will have had a bitter experience with all of sin's deplorable consequences. Yet when Satan is loosed, he will find those who have a hidden sympathy for sin, ready to be beguiled by his deceptions. All those who do not love the Lord supremely will cease to exist, while all whose lives demonstrate the purity of love in their hearts will have their names written in the Lamb's Book of Life. They will be given an entrance into the New Jerusalem, which has come to earth for the victors.

The promises of the Bible are ultimately for the overcomers both in the Christian Age and the Millennial Age.

Preface

Though all live knowing death is inevitable, death is an unaccepted reality. Only those in pain or suffering welcome it as a relief. Life was meant to be lived to its fullest as long as men have breath. The mind finds it difficult to accept the reality of death. People want desperately to believe that life will never cease. The truth of the regeneration will make clear that life is very real, but so is death.

What was not generally known, although it should have been because of clear scriptural statements, is that "all in the graves shall hear his voice, and shall come forth" (John 5:28, 29). There was, in some cases, a certain feeling of relief believing that all sins, hurt, and pain were buried with each person. As much as mankind has hated the reality of death, nonetheless, they have liked the idea of having their dark deeds buried with them. When their eyes closed all their actions would be locked in the grave, or so they thought. The period of regeneration, however, is a time lock waiting to be opened as soon as people return to life. The opening of the grave will yield every secret and hidden thing—all will be brought to light again.

Being made alive again is the most wonderful gift imaginable. Men did nothing to receive life in the first place, nor anything to receive it again. Both are gifts from God. Many who squandered their first life will return wiser and more determined to make good the second time around.

In our past stories, we looked into different lives to see both the joys and heartaches that living again brought. When former evil behaviors awakened with mankind, this had a painful aspect to it. However, those who chose to make things right found it possible to do so. Many times the mistakes of the past became stepping-stones to higher and nobler ground. Even when one had committed serious violations against righteousness, being reconciled to his fellows was still possible if he was willing to do so. Every effort to repair the mistakes of the past helped build character, and character is what the regeneration is all about. Christ could restore life, but he could not bestow character upon those who lacked it. Character has to be developed with will and determination along with heavenly grace.

Our story continues toward the end of the thousand years of Christ's reign. People have long since been reconciled to their fellow human beings, but the hardest part of living again was being reconciled to a God, who by His nature, has zero tolerance for sin. Throughout the centuries of its existence, mankind has prided itself in tolerance for sin, having "broadminded" ways of viewing the circumstances surrounding sin, and became increasingly comfortable with it. Outrage was diminished. "Understanding" *why* a sin was committed somehow made it acceptable, with minimal or absence of rebuke and correction.

The world in the regeneration changed all of this. Suddenly there were no soft euphemisms for sin. Sin was recognized for what it always was—evil and deserving of death. The refining processes of Christ had been steadily at work throughout his reign, and at last mankind began to resemble the pure perfection of Adam and Eve before they sinned. The work of the Mediator in cleansing the hearts of the billions of earth had been an incredible work. Change had never come easily for people, but bringing them from total defilement into the "image of God" was the most difficult challenge of all.

Two overall conditions of character developed in the hearts of a certain segment of humanity during this great rule of righteousness. All had managed to break sinful habits and to walk with remarkable discipline in the right paths. However, one class, while abstaining from sin, also found it unnecessary to reach out to others. Only when required to give themselves in service would they do so. If service was not requested, they found reasons to indulge in the various pleasures of life. Another class could and did give themselves in service for others, but in the recesses of their hearts there remained a desire for things forbidden. This desire, while outwardly appearing almost dead, lay dormant, waiting until it heard the familiar voice of the devil once he was released from his "binding" in the abyss.

The thousand years will end with two separate trials: (1) The separation of the "sheep" from the "goats" who will be condemned by sins of omission and, (2) rebellion that will become a sin of commission while enlisting under Satan's banner. It is only then that the names of those written in the Lamb's Book of Life will be known, and only such, having passed all tests of character, will gain entrance as citizens into the New Jerusalem. Since the whole period of Christ's reign had been a testing time, some will be surprised to find that they failed to have their names recorded in the most important book of all—the Lamb's Book of Life. Only those who love the "Lord thy God with all thy heart, and with all thy soul, and with all thy mind" will stand triumphant before the "great white throne" (Matthew 22:37; Revelation 20:11).

In this book we take up life toward the close of the Millennium and then into the "little season," when Satan is loosed from his prison (Revelation 20:7). We will walk along with our old friends, Lev and his former wife, Rebekah.

*"Even in laughter the heart is sorrowful;
and the end of that mirth is heaviness"
(Proverbs 14:13).*

Chapter One

Lev was excited about meeting Rebekah in Hawaii on their return from assignments in Japan and Australia. They had not seen each other in months and were looking forward to being together on the Islands, where he had made accommodations for two cottages along the oceanfront.

As his plane touched down on the Big Island, Lev was reminded how Hawaii's beauty was enhanced a hundredfold now. Commercialism had been replaced by a return to the lush abundance of the natural features for which the Hawaiian Islands had always been known. Eager to see Rebekah again, he strolled over to the tarmac where the Australian plane was due to set down in half an hour. Both Lev and Rebekah looked young and vibrant, with only their eyes revealing their centuries of maturity. Wisdom and grace could not be hidden there.

He watched as the plane landed effortlessly. His heart jumped when he saw Rebekah's radiant face, her eyes searching the crowd for him. They embraced in heartfelt joy, not saying a word. At last Rebekah said, "Lev, I enjoyed my work in Australia, but I was glad when it was finished so I could see you again."

"I know what you mean, Rebekah," laughed Lev. "It's true— absence makes the heart grow fonder! We can relax together before we return home. My guess is this island has more varieties of fruit than any place in the world. But anywhere we go today, we're never away from the trees of life."

"That sounds wonderful, Lev. I would love to lie in the sand for awhile and then take a long swim with you."

"Me too! I have a car to use while we're here. Allow me to chauffeur you around, madam!"

"I'm ready!" She smiled with pleasure.

Majestic Beauty Everywhere

They drove a very comfortable car to the charming, blue-shuttered cottages. As they went along the seaside, rolling waves were lapping the shore driven by a light breeze. It was only midmorning, but already the beach was sprinkled with people enjoying the warm sun and sparkling surf. Long ago, there would have been both slender and heavy people, short and tall, old and young. Now, everyone was young and vibrant, physically perfect, and exceptionally attractive. The ocean-scented air was clean and invigorating.

"Here we are at last, Rebekah. Your cottage is over there. When you freshen up and change, I'll be waiting for you at the beachfront. See the large red umbrella? That's ours. I have iced tea and a basket of fruit waiting for us. See you there!"

Lev changed quickly and carried the snacks out to the cotton blanket under the beach umbrella. No sooner had he arranged everything than a handsome man with a golden tan invited him to a volleyball game. Lev thanked him but declined, explaining that they were planning to rest and then have a long swim. "We're here for a short stopover and wanted time to catch up on our lives."

The man seemed vaguely annoyed. "Oh, you're not one of those people too busy to enjoy life are you? Take time out and live a little! Besides, we need a few more people for our game. How about it? By the way, my name is Henry Edgar."

"Pleased to meet you, Henry. I'm Lev Aron. I'll wait until my friend comes and see what she wants to do. I suppose a little volleyball might be good exercise. You're asking the wrong people if you're expecting us to be strong competitors. We've had little time for sports."

"Aha!" Henry exclaimed. "So you *are* one of those people!"

Lev nodded with a smile. "I guess so, but I doubt anyone enjoys life more than we do, because there is so much pleasure in helping others. It's exciting to make the earth the paradise it was intended to be."

"That's great, but as they say, 'a little nonsense now and then is relished by the best of men,'" Henry quipped.

Soon Rebekah appeared looking as cheerful and charming as ever. It was her lovely eyes that revealed years of experience, discipline, and love for God and fellow man. No sooner had she reclined than Henry appeared again, inviting them both to join in their game. Lev introduced Rebekah to him.

"Pleased to meet you, ma'am. I hope you are more enthusiastic for a good game than your friend, here. We really need a couple of more people to make our game interesting. What do you say?"

"It's not exactly what I had in mind, but I suppose a little exercise might be relaxing. How about you, Lev?"

"All right, it's your call, Rebekah. I'm game if you are."

"Give us ten minutes to have some tea and fruit, and then we'll be ready, Henry."

"You're on! Ten minutes is fine. I'll round up the troops."

Lev and Rebekah sipped a little juice while looking out on the vast expanse of the ocean and the relaxing waves. Aware of their commitment, they decided to wait until after their exercise to enjoy the array of fruit.

Henry soon motioned to them, and after brief introductions it was decided that Lev and Rebekah would play on opposite sides. The ball went back and forth over the net at a fast pace. Everyone played with exceptional skill except the two new recruits. However, considering that they had not played for several centuries, they both did reasonably well. The score was close, but at the last moment Lev was in the right place at the right moment, enabling his team to take the last point. "Beginner's luck!" he shouted good-naturedly.

An Excuse to Party

Exhilarated from the play, the crowd insisted their two new friends join them that night at a gathering to be held on the beach. Lev and Rebekah tried to decline, hoping to spend some quiet time together, sharing experiences and how the providences in their lives had helped to increase their character growth.

Henry persisted. "Lev, you made the winning point, so don't spoil our little celebration tonight. You made the point fair and square! For someone who claims no practice, you outdid yourself. You must be our guest of honor!"

"Not really," Lev demurred. "I just happened to be standing there when the ball came my way. You were going to have this party anyway, no matter who won or lost. Why don't you go ahead and have your party? We will be leaving probably tomorrow, so we are not going to be a part of your team. From the look of your tans, you must have been on these beaches for quite some time."

"We have been learning to relax a little while vacationing. Most of us have taken care of all our responsibilities, so we decided to take a long holiday. That's what you both need to do. You need to loosen up and unwind a little," Henry asserted. "You can have your long swim this afternoon and be back by eight this evening. We have music, refreshments, and lots of good clean fun. We are even having a fish cookout, Hawaiian style. I'll bet you haven't tasted fish like this in ages. How about it? Don't be a wet blanket!"

Rebekah said, "Oh, all right. It sounds inviting. How about it, Lev?"

Since Rebekah had half accepted, Lev didn't have the heart to turn everyone down. "Okay, if you say so."

As they left to take their long swim, Lev said, "I'm not sure, but I have the feeling we are contributing to someone's misbehavior. Maybe I'm out of line, but it looks to me like Henry and his friends think it's time to sit back and enjoy themselves, while there is still much work to be done. Everyone does need a little recreation once in a while to refuel, but these people are obsessed with having a good time. This idea that 'I have fulfilled my responsibilities, therefore I am supposed to settle down to a life of good times and endless play' seems a little strange to me."

Always one to see the good in others, Rebekah cautioned, "Oh, Lev, you push yourself too hard and you expect others to do likewise. Maybe they're just taking a few weeks off before taking on some additional tasks."

"Maybe you're right," Lev sighed. "Anyway, let's swim out to the one-mile buoy and back. Remember, don't get too far away from me. I checked and the tide won't be going out until later this evening, so we should be safe."

"I'd rather swim to the half-mile buoy and then swim parallel to the shore for a bit. It would be swimming the same distance, but it's always best to be on the safe side. Okay? Last one into the water has to fix breakfast tomorrow."

Rebekah got in first, diving into a rolling wave. They swam lazily, reaching the half-mile buoy without effort. The wind was picking up, and the waves were getting bigger. They had to be careful not to get hit by one of the surfboarders who had joined them in the water. They were about to turn back to shore when they noticed an empty surfboard floating nearby.

"Lev, look!" cried Rebekah as she searched the surface for the rider.

"You look for him on the surface, while I go underwater looking for someone. He must be somewhere in the water!" Lev shouted.

Catching a good breath, Lev went under. Fortunately, the water was clean and visibility was good. Sure enough, he spotted a man about twenty feet away struggling to reach the surface. Lev reached him about the same time he managed to take a breath of air. He was sputtering and gasping.

"Are you all right, sir?"

A New Friend

"I think so—but please stay close if you wouldn't mind. I swallowed a little water. I was just learning to surf and lost my balance. Unfortunately, I didn't have time to catch my breath before going under, so I was in trouble right away. Then I made another mistake and started swimming under the water. The rolling waves mixed me up, and I panicked. Thanks for coming after me."

Meanwhile, Rebekah had grabbed his surfboard and swam, pushing it toward them. "Get on. This will make your trip to shore a lot easier. We'll swim alongside to keep you company," she said.

He gratefully climbed on board, still coughing up water while they pushed him toward shore. Safely on land, he said, "Thank you, again. I needed that help and I appreciate everything you did for me. I wasn't drowning, but it was very uncomfortable! I was really glad for your assistance. My name is Craig Glover," reaching out his hand to Lev first.

"Pleased to meet you, Craig. I'm Lev Aron, and this is my dearest friend, Rebekah. We're just spending a couple days here and decided to take a little swim. I'm glad we were there to help you out."

"I was returning from a project I have been working on in China," Craig volunteered, "and thought I could catch a day or two in the sun. Surfing looked so easy, so I thought I'd give it a try. I guess the old adage, 'Everything looks easier to do than it is,' still holds true even at this end of the age."

"I know what you mean! Looking at those experts out there makes it look so easy to do. They ride the waves like they were standing on solid ground. They really shouldn't have given you a surfboard without checking to see if you had any experience. You probably should have had a trainer before venturing out by yourself."

"You're absolutely right, Lev! Thanks, again, to both of you. I'm going to rest up awhile and take in the beach party this evening. Will you be there?"

"Yes, we will be going, even though I'm not entirely comfortable about it. I got the impression that having fun is the main focus of some who are going tonight," Lev mentioned.

"You know, that was my reaction, too, Lev. I don't know why, but they talked as if they were going from one kind of party to another. Everybody needs a little rest, but we aren't here just to relax, are we?"

Rebekah chided gently. "We really don't know that much about these people. They certainly are friendly to strangers. We should appreciate that."

"That is true," Craig agreed. "Perhaps we are overlooking what they have done. If we knew more, we might have a better opinion of them. I shouldn't be so quick to judge. Anyway, thanks again for bringing me in on that surfboard. That was one of the best rides I've ever had! I'll see you tonight, then."

Lev and Rebekah lay back in the warm sand until evening, relaxing, talking, and enjoying the magical beauty of being together on this paradise island. Time seemed to stand still. Brilliant hues of the sunset danced across the water as they watched the huge red sun sink into the horizon. Every day, the wonderment of earth's glory increased.

The evening came too quickly, and soon they found themselves leaving for the gathering. They arrived about the same time as Craig did, and he latched onto them as to long-lost friends.

The three new guests were impressed with the lavish party atmosphere. Musicians were playing captivating melodies and the tables were set with every artistic fruit display imaginable. When preparations were complete, Henry asked Lev, as the pronounced guest of honor, to ask the blessing on the food. Everything was so elegant and festive that it was a night to remember. The moon had risen and its reflection danced on the water.

Rebekah whispered to Lev, "This is too lovely for words. Perhaps we should extend our stay here."

Inviting Their Delay

Henry either heard her whisper or he was a lip reader, for he came right over. "Now you are coming to your senses. What is the hurry? We have forever now, don't we?"

Soon he was back serving plates of hot steaming fish, cooked in special juices. The portions were generous, and everyone had worked up a good appetite during the day.

After the sumptuous meal, Henry stood up as the master of ceremonies. He called on Lev Aron to join him as the one who had won the game for his side that day. "Let's give Lev a hand! How about a few words from our hero for the day?"

Lev blushed because it seemed so superficial. The score he made was almost an accident, and everyone knew that. Not wishing to be a spoilsport on such a pleasant occasion, Lev chose his words carefully.

"Thank you, Henry, and everyone who prepared this wonderful evening. Rebekah and I are overwhelmed with your hospitality. We have been very busy trying to perfect some of the processes that make life so comfortable, so we thought we would spend a day here in Hawaii on our way home to Israel for another assignment. This evening has been wonderful. Thank you very much for including us.

"Let me also encourage you, as your vacations come to an end, to stay focused. It has been said that 'on the plains of hesitation lie the bones of countless thousands, who on the dawn of victory, sat down to rest, and resting died.' Until our names are written in the Lamb's Book of Life, we do well not to relax too long or to make merry for more than a moment. Let us accept the disciplines of the time being afforded us. This is still a day of judgment and only those who are overcomers will have their names written in the Lamb's Book of Life."

Craig applauded loudly, saying, "Amen, Lev. These are my sentiments exactly."

Henry caught the little correction in Lev's message, but he graciously thanked him.

"Thank you, Lev. We are always grateful for reminders to press on. We all have given our time and effort generously in the great regeneration program. If our Lord has a need of any kind, we will eagerly minister to it. We are caring and sensitive people. Until we get new assignments, we are enjoying the blessings the Lord has abundantly provided. We wish you Godspeed on your new assignments, Lev and Rebekah. Again, thank you for sharing this day with us."

Craig asked to say a few words.

"Yes, please do," Henry responded.

Craig stood formally since it seemed to be the structure of this part of the event.

"This has been a mixed day, of sorts. I thought I would try a little surfing in the Hawaiian Ocean—a new experience for me! It looked so easy!" He laughed at his own naiveté. "Anyway, to make my story short, I was swallowing more ocean water than I had planned. Fortunately, Lev and Rebekah were nearby to lend a hand to a surfer in trouble. Of course, I would have survived somehow without their help, but it was their eagerness to assist me that impressed me. I shall remember it always as an act of love and kindness—a bonding of human spirit.

"This evening also has been exceptionally warm and gracious to someone who is a total stranger traveling through for a day. It was the perfect ending for an exceptional day. I thank you for it. However, of my two experiences this day, I shall remember the first one forever, because I was glad for the help in my time of need. The earth still has needs even though no one is hungry or without lodging. We were told to 'fill the earth and subdue it.' We have filled it rather well, but are we still trying to undo the damage of six thousand years of human exploitation? Until we have fulfilled our commission, we should not rest on our laurels. Thank you."

There was an awkward silence. Then the musicians filled the air with their beautiful music again. It was plain to see that no one was particularly responsive to Lev and Craig's comments about the needs that still existed worldwide. The beach party people were going to enjoy their festivities, while others were going to continue subduing the earth and caring for human needs, opportunity by opportunity.

Impatience for Good Times

As the evening ended, Craig paused to thank Lev and Rebekah again for their kindness and also for Lev's words of encouragement. While they walked along the beach toward their cottages, Craig said, "I was slightly uncomfortable about tonight's festivities. If it were just a passing occasion, I wouldn't have that feeling I am sure. Somehow, however, I am afraid that this attitude is growing among some people. There is almost an impatience to 'get on with the good times.' Is this just my impression, or did you get that feeling, too?"

Rebekah said, "I like to give people the benefit of the doubt, but I did feel an uneasiness, too. There certainly wasn't anything wrong happening, but it could be argued that it is less than the ideal way to show our commitment to the King. Since he has undertaken the task of mediating between God and man, the least we can do is not leave a stone unturned in getting everyone ready to stand before the Judge of All."

"Precisely the point, Rebekah. Some people's hearts seem filled with kindness and graciousness, but they still miss the point," Craig mused.

"I could not agree more," Lev interjected. "What is happening is that love is turning inward. I think that is what stumbled mother Eve. She felt that realms of light and knowledge were being withheld from her—worlds that the angels enjoyed, so why shouldn't she? It wasn't perverse or evil, but it only took a little disobedience to set off a chain reaction that the human race experienced for the next six thousand years. The moment she failed to obey God, she demonstrated that she did not love Him supremely. One cannot love God in an absolute sense and disobey Him. That is not possible."

Craig chimed in, "That is so true, Lev! I am afraid it is very dangerous if we are ending the time of Christ's reign as Mediator, but loving pleasure and self more than God or our fellow man. Fortunately, I don't see this as pervasive in most communities. I am sure you both have traveled as much or more than I—what is your assessment?"

"When I travel," Rebekah explained, "it is mostly to help out with projects that need another hand. So most of the people I am with are giving of themselves freely and under these conditions. I don't see this nonstop party spirit."

"I ran into it early in the regeneration, but we were able to point the people in a better direction," Lev added. "However, just recently, I have noticed it again. I don't know, in this case, whether it is just a momentary diversion or whether it runs deeper than that. But it is not a healthy sign. When things are pleasant and running smoothly for so long, it is easy to conclude there is time to enjoy life in a more self-centered way."

"I am glad that you spoke so earnestly, Lev. I think many people feel they have done what was asked of them and they are virtually assured of eternal life. It is easy to conclude that, because they are good and caring people," Craig said. "They function on a very high level of nobility, but it gives them a false sense of security. Anyway, some things are not in our power to fix, are they?"

"Yes, that is true, Craig," Lev concluded.

"Well, Lev and Rebekah, it has been a pleasure meeting you and thank you again for your kindness and help out there in the ocean. I hope we will meet again. I live in England, but perhaps I'll get down to Israel some day."

"If you do, be sure to look us up, Craig. We'll be glad to see you any time. You may not be entertained as extravagantly as tonight, but it will be genuine hospitality just the same," Lev added as they shook hands.

The next day Lev and Rebekah caught a plane to Israel, eager to be home again for a season. No one met them at the airport, so they secured a small aircraft to fly home. Everything was so tranquil that it almost didn't seem normal.

"And when the thousand years are expired"
(Revelation 20:7).

Chapter Two

Rebekah arrived at her house to find a visitor living there. This was a common occurrence, and houses were often occupied while the owners were away. When owners left their homes, they informed the community leaders and invited any travelers in the area to make use of their facilities. This is what Rebekah had done.

Seeing the lights on in her home in the evening, she rang the bell before entering. A cheerful lady greeted her.

"Welcome home, Rebekah! My name is Holly Welles. I have been staying in your home while you were gone and appreciate it so much! I would like to stay a few more days, if that would be okay with you."

"I am delighted to meet you, Holly. I hope you have made yourself comfortable. I was living similarly in Australia for nearly two months, so I think the idea of sharing our homes is great. Don't let me interrupt what you're doing. You are a welcome guest and everything here is at your disposal. Which bedroom are you using? I'll take the other one. That way no one will have to move."

"I have been using the guest room opposite your bedroom. You must be tired, Rebekah. Would you like a cup of tea and some fruit before turning in?"

"Sure, that sounds great! I am tired from traveling and will probably go to bed early this evening. After I freshen up a bit, I'll join you."

Soon Rebekah appeared, asking, "What brings you to Israel, Holly?"

"My answer might surprise you, but I have come here to learn, if I can, when the thousand years of Christ reign began in order to get some idea as to when it will end."

"Have you been able to find an answer to your question?"

"No—the longer and deeper I search, the more unfathomable it seems. Some say the end of Christ's reign is close at hand. Others say it is another hundred years away, and others even say two hundred. So I am more confused than when I first arrived here."

"Did you ask for an audience with the Ancient Worthies?"

"Yes, and I spoke to Abraham, Sarah, and Joseph, but they said they couldn't reveal that information to me. They are amazing people, and I was so enthralled meeting them, but obviously this information is not available for publication."

"Did that end your search?"

"No, but I guess I'm no closer to an answer than before I came."

"Why not just accept that they won't reveal it to you?"

"Some people back home in the States have projected some starting dates, and if some of them are true, it seems we are almost at the end of the thousand years."

"You know, Eve got in trouble desiring knowledge that was off limits. I think it is better to learn from her mistake. It will end when it will end."

"I guess I still have Eve's curiosity. I thought the knowledge was around, and all I had to do was scratch a little here and there to find it."

The Quest for Knowledge

"What would you do with it if you had it?"

Holly thought for a moment, and then chuckled. "I suppose I would go around with a gleam in my eye. Probably no one would believe me if I had the answer. My curiosity would be satisfied at least, if I *knew* the answer."

"Well, Holly, I am afraid you are going to have to be satisfied not knowing," Rebekah said with a smile. "If the Ancients won't reveal it, my advice would be to leave it alone. I am sure they know but are forbidden to make the information available."

"That is what I was told back home. I have been exposed to various unofficial views on the matter, and some of them seem highly probable. I thought with a little effort on my part I could find the official answer. I guess my visit was in vain."

"No, not if you leave wiser than when you came. We all know that the truth will be revealed when the proper time comes. Until then it is all right to work with different figures, but only what is revealed belongs to us."

"Yes, Rebekah. You are right. I feel a little frustrated, because I thought this wasn't going to be a secret."

"It won't be once the devil is let out of the 'abyss.' We will know that the thousand years have expired then, won't we?"

"I was once a reporter, so I thought I could come up with a great scoop. I will just have to give up on this idea." Holly sat back contentedly and sipped her tea. "Now that I think of it, I must have seemed pushy and irreverent to the Ancients. Not that I was disrespectful, but it was bold of me to be so inquisitive. I should have known that this matter would be revealed at the proper time without the likes of me intruding into it."

"Don't worry, Holly. They are the kindest and most gracious of all people. Didn't you find them extraordinary in every way?"

"Oh, yes! I just loved them, Rebekah. They treated me so gently, when they could have been rather stern with me. I think I deserved to be asked to leave."

"Every time I have been with them, I have left with goose bumps. They are simply the best thing that has happened in the way of leadership. I have never heard anyone yet complain about their leadership. Without a question, they are truly great. This is the first time in history when we have had perfect planning and government. No mistakes and nothing to do over. Everything they have done has prospered. We are certainly in their debt."

"Yes," Holly agreed. "And the worst of it is, most people don't know how dedicated they have been. They have been working around the clock since they assumed the leadership of this world. Of course, behind these great people is our Lord. To him goes the glory and honor for all the wonderful things that have taken place in this world. I guess I must be keeping you up. I know you are tired from traveling, so don't feel that you have to entertain me, Rebekah. I have so much enjoyed talking to you. I only wish I had spoken to you before I made a fool of myself with the Ancients."

"Don't worry, Holly. It is all a part of the process. I was quite tired, but talking to you kind of awakened me. I do think I'll leave the thousand years alone for now. I have heard others voice concern about their ending date, but I think keeping it unknown is a part of the test being placed upon mankind."

"That is interesting! I didn't realize so many were asking the same question!"

"Well, I guess I will go to bed after all. I will see you in the morning, Holly. Thanks for taking care of my house and plants while I was away. By the way, Lev, my former husband, and I are going up to Jerusalem for a meeting with the Ancients. Would you like to come with us?"

"I would be delighted at the privilege, but I'm afraid they will throw me out on my ear if they see me again."

Rebekah laughed. "Have no fear of that. We'll take in the chapel meeting, and then after a quick breakfast we will fly up to Jerusalem."

"Great! I'll be ready. This is such an unexpected privilege. Thank you!"

Visiting the Holy City

The next morning after breakfast, they left for Jerusalem. Holly was excited to be meeting the Ancients once again, hoping that they weren't offended by her first visit. The flight from Beersheba to Jerusalem was a short hop. They were ushered into a meeting with several Ancients arranged by Moses, Elijah, and Joseph. Lev and Rebekah were received as old friends, and Holly was warmly greeted with affection.

Moses said, "We appreciated both of you going to Japan and Australia to help with technical matters, but now we want you to work on a more sensitive mission. As you know, there has been a lot of speculation with regard to the end of the thousand years." At this, Holly blushed and tried to appear smaller in her seat.

"Not only so, but because people have lived through so many centuries, they are beginning to feel it is time to relax and seek pleasure, believing that the work has been accomplished and that they have demonstrated that they are entitled to have their name in the Lamb's Book of Life. Admittedly, this is a small minority in society, but they are cropping up here and there and need to be reminded that this is not the way to achieve success in character development."

Lev replied, "Yes, we stayed over in Hawaii and found a group of beachgoers who felt they had done their share and now was the time for life to be a nonstop party."

"So, what did you do?" asked Joseph.

"You know Lev," Rebekah reported. "He thanked them for their hospitality and then told them to stay focused on the goals of the regeneration."

"Good," nodded Elijah. "People do not realize that gaining eternal life will require enormous effort to demonstrate that they love God supremely. Without a burning love for God and our fellow men, they stand in danger of falling short."

Rebekah commented, "There have been so many changes from the past that some do not realize how high God's standards of perfection are. No one is hungry, and no one is living in the street. For this reason, they do not see needs anywhere and are blind to other ways they can serve the well-being of the community. It is easier to gravitate to the good times."

"Yes," Lev agreed. "Even more disconcerting is the preoccupation with the question of when the thousand years will end. No one gave much thought to it when Christ returned to earth, except those few watchful Christians living around that time. Now many are trying to pinpoint the date when he will turn the kingdom over to the Father. Why people concern themselves with Christ's business is strange indeed. They should be concerned about their own character attainments and eagerness to serve the common good."

Holly finally gathered the courage to speak up. "I plead guilty and am so ashamed of myself. I came to Israel thinking I would get the inside scoop on when Christ's reign will end. I understand now how presumptuous that is and promise to mind my own affairs. Please forgive me."

Joseph gave her an approving smile. "Good! We all seem to be on track here, so let's get down to the business at hand. There have been pockets of people throughout Europe who are extremely interested in the subject of when Christ will step out of his office as Mediator between God and man. The things that are revealed belong to man. The things not revealed belong to God. It is that simple. However, some are not willing to leave it be and want to be the first to solve the question of when Christ's reign ends. So when you meet with them, never debate their figures nor become engaged in these discussions."

"What should we do?" Lev asked.

Moses immediately advised. "They should be asked if they are eager for Satan to be loosed from the abyss. That is one of the things that will happen when the thousand years are ended. At the same time, Jesus will cease mediating between God and man. It will be a very critical time as they will no longer have the protection of a Mediator. However, some may not make it past the thousand years if they don't learn to love God and their fellow man in a more meaningful way."

Still Time to Renew Diligence

Elijah added, "We are approaching the end of this age, and before it is ended there will be a separation of the 'sheep' from the 'goats,' as our Lord predicted. There is still time for those who have been a little remiss to renew their diligence. And that is what your mission is, Lev and Rebekah. Try to fan the flames of love in hearts that may have become a little cold. Our aim is to make sure that everyone is given all the help needed to achieve everlasting life. God desires that all have a full opportunity for life."

Lev replied, "We are at the service of our King. We have come expecting to accept whatever assignment you may have for us. We tremble at the thought that any should fail, especially having come this far."

Moses nodded. "Good, we are grateful for your willing hearts. You will be traveling first to France and subsequently to Switzerland. In a community outside of what was once Paris, there is a company of people who have turned toward pleasure. They are convinced that all the work has been done. Mingle with that company and see if you can influence them in changing their attitude. People are free to do what they want, but they are not free from the consequences of their actions. Remember, the 'goats' are condemned for the sins of *omission* and not the sins of commission (Matthew 25:31-45). One can fail to gain life because of what they *don't* do. Actions are indicators of our heart condition. You will have your instructions handed to you at the front desk as you leave. We wish you Godspeed, Shalom."

As they turned to leave, Joseph addressed Holly. Putting his hand gently on her shoulder, he kindly said, "You are in good company with Lev and Rebekah, Holly, so watch them very carefully and try to emulate their actions."

"Thank you, sir. I needed correction badly. I am thankful to have been pointed to the better path. I have learned a great deal from them in just a short while. Thank you. Shalom."

Lev and Rebekah picked up their assignments at the front desk and proceeded to their aircraft. They were surprised they would both be going to the same communities as visiting tourists. The first visit would be to a small community called Basel not very far from Paris.

Stopping at Basel

The next morning, after bidding farewell to Holly, Lev and Rebekah prepared for their new mission. They flew into Paris, securing a small aircraft to continue to Basel. They had been given accommodations in homes of people who were out of town working on different projects. Landing on the pad of Franz Eberhardt, Lev carried Rebekah's things inside.

"I'll land at another pad down the road about a block away to unload my things. When I return, we can have supper together. I'll be staying at Vernon Boleur's home. He is in the States taking care of some matters. We should be moving on before they get back. If you get invited to any type of activity for the evening, please include me in the arrangements. We will try to be as gregarious as we can, to learn the thinking of the people here. See you shortly."

No sooner had Rebekah unpacked her things than the doorbell rang. At the door stood a most gracious lady. "Hello! I am here to welcome you to our little community. My name is Naomi

Gishard. We hope you enjoy your stay here. We are having a musical and poetry meeting at my home this evening—the first house to your left. It starts at eight o'clock. Won't you please come?"

"Yes! Thank you, Naomi. My former husband, Lev Aron, is just down the road. Would it be rude of me to bring him along?"

"Of course not! We would be delighted to have you both. The name Lev Aron brings back memories of the early days when he helped change our industrial output to conform to the new standards being introduced. It was pretty technical at the time, I still remember. My father worked with Lev and speaks so highly of him. Isn't it amazing that we can remember back hundreds of years now? Oh, I do hope he will come! Having you both with us will add special interest to our gathering. Thank you for accepting! I must hurry along to get everything in order for the evening. We'll see you at eight! Shalom."

Rebekah was pleased that they were noticed and invited to share in the neighborhood activities. By the time Lev arrived, she had time to arrange a lovely meal. Lev was grateful that no time was being wasted, and they would have an opportunity to meet with the community people.

Lev and Rebekah arrived a few minutes before eight to find a house full of guests, seemingly blessed with numerous talents. Naomi Gishard welcomed them graciously and Rebekah introduced Lev.

"I am so happy to meet you, Mr. Aron. I learned about you from my father when I was a little girl. He speaks so well of you. He said you seemed to have the answer for everything. Yes, I do believe you are a most remarkable man just by looking at you."

Naomi then took Lev and Rebekah around to different ones for introductions. Then it was time to announce the activities of the evening. They would have a small orchestra play music that had just been written. This would be followed by half an hour of poetry, ending the evening with refreshments and fellowship.

Soon the orchestra started playing music of rare beauty. Lev learned later that the writers of the music had been professional musicians, and this music was a part of an upcoming concert. The two Israelis closed their eyes as the enchanting music filled the room. The time passed quickly, and soon the poetry began. The poems were noble and pure, filled with praise for Christ and all he had done for mankind. It was all very stimulating. Rebekah wished she had such incredible musical talents.

An Offer of Preferred Seats

Naomi was the perfect hostess, making sure that Lev and Rebekah were served from the vast array of refreshments. The writer of the music, and apparently the lead musician, invited Lev and Rebekah to a concert to be held on the weekend. He introduced himself, "My name is Ernest Gishard. I am the former husband of Naomi, our charming hostess of the evening. If you mention my name, I will have you ushered to the most preferred seats in the house. It is a privilege to have both of you with us. Naomi has told us of your brilliant accomplishments in the early days of this regeneration program."

"Thank you for your kind offer. We will plan on being at your concert. We enjoyed this evening very much. We seldom have such relaxation, so it has really been a treat for us to join you."

"Maybe you are too busy, Monsieur. One must take time to smell the flowers and enjoy life."

"Oh, we are not *that* busy. I do not know that anyone enjoys life more than we do. We have met so many dedicated people that we are always inspired by their untiring love and devotion. Loving God and loving people make life so fulfilling for us. Life becomes sweeter even though we carry a heavy workload. There is a sense of accomplishment in improving the way things are done, making them better in every way."

"Yes, but isn't enough, enough? It has been beautiful for many years! Isn't it time for us to start to enjoy the fruits of our labor and sacrifices?" asked Ernest, as he rested back on Naomi's deeply cushioned floral sofa.

Lev realized that an opportunity was opening to fulfill the mission he had been given.

"Well," Lev chose his words carefully, "When Christ says, 'Come ye, blessed of my Father, inherit the kingdom prepared for you from the foundation of the world' (Matthew 25:34), he seems to refer to the time that we enter into the joys of the Lord. Until that blessed time, shouldn't we have love that labors and faith that works? Besides, serving others is already a joy of the Lord. Failing in this, we may not be in that class invited to inherit the kingdom."

"I must say, that sounds very altruistic," Ernest acknowledged. "However, when we provide beautiful music and fine arts to lift people up, isn't that a blessing and uplift to mankind?"

"Oh, yes, indeed that is. That is a much-needed service. God made man to appreciate music. After all, He is a God of music. However, music is only one of mankind's needs. We all have more than one capacity in which to serve mankind. We are multi-talented and can easily serve in a host of ways to bless mankind and subdue this world."

Rebekah joined the discussion. "We did enjoy the evening. Your music seems to echo strains from heaven. We will look forward to hearing more. Thank you for your gracious invitation."

Ernest turned to Rebekah. "Tell me about some of your assignments."

"I would be delighted. Lev and I have had the privilege of working on all kinds of projects. Some in the sciences, some with people in unique situations, some regarding nature, some in the common tasks of planting and building. I think we have worn every kind of hat in our happy years of service. It is love that makes life magic. Without love, we would be eating, breathing and living without a purpose."

"I must say I am fascinated with your tireless devotion to God and mankind. Perhaps I need to emulate your spirit in my activities. I suppose I have just settled down with what I love most, and that is music. You are right, though, it is love that makes life sweet. Without love it would be 'Music played in empty halls, that echoes against hollow walls, with no one there to hear it.' Yes, you are right."

Naomi listened carefully, catching the implications of their conversation. "Do you think, Lev, that possibly we should still be given to a greater breadth of activities? I am asking this very earnestly. We do not want to be considered as the 'goats' in that parable you quoted. Should we be giving ourselves to additional works for the common good of mankind? I know many people who never seem to cease working. They take on project after project. I can see that you both are that type, and I admire it. It does require selfless giving and tireless sacrifices, even though as you say, the reward comes back in having greater love for God and mankind."

Character and Works

Lev smiled inwardly. "It is not for me to tell other people what to do. I don't wish to convey any thought that salvation comes through works. Salvation comes through a character that loves mankind and loves God supremely. But there is a correlation between character and works. It is possible to work with wrong motivation. If work is without love, it is absolutely meaningless. However, true love labors and true faith works. Christ will soon separate the 'sheep' from the 'goats.' It is not for me to presume who are 'sheep' and who are 'goats.' The narrative of the parable seems to indicate that those who *actively* serve Christ's brethren out of love will pass the test. That is a safe observation, and we do well to consider it very carefully."

Ernest Gishard remained quiet before venturing an answer. Finally, he said, "Lev, I think you and Rebekah have made your point very well. Without a doubt we will be well-advised to get back on track by more devotion and activities beyond our music in contributing to the common good of mankind. I am grateful for this conversation. I must admit we have developed blind spots and have been acting more like 'goats' than 'sheep.'"

"Ernest, I hope nothing I said was directed at implicating you as such. When you create beautiful music, you are certainly beautifying the hearts and minds of people. We need that. God made us with the capacity to create music and to enjoy it. I am sure God Himself is the author of beautiful music. However, in this critical time, the enjoyment of music should probably be subordinate to some of the more immediate needs we face. Christ has successfully accomplished the return of the entire human race. Everyone is rich and completely provided for. This was accomplished through the labor of billions. But we still have work to do in subduing the earth and making it comparable to the Paradise in Eden. Rebekah and I have paused to rest and refresh ourselves from time to time, but we have always felt that as long as there are needs, we should be active in addressing them. One of the best ways we can help others is by example."

Most of those in attendance that evening were listening intently to their conversation. Their quiet thoughtfulness in paying attention was gratifying to Rebekah and Lev. In this rather pleasant discussion, most of those present desired to focus on personal responsibility.

About the time it seemed that guests were all in agreement and some were preparing to head home, a man who had been silent all evening spoke up.

"My name is Alfred Destrie, and I find myself disturbed by the discussions of this evening. Somehow, I think we are being asked to labor and sacrifice where no necessity exists. We are good people. Look at what transformation of character has taken place from what we once were to where we are now. We have made astonishing progress. We have attained great heights of character. Yet somehow, to our new friends, that is not enough. Why is it not enough? Will anything ever be enough? We must seemingly be driven to do more, to be more. What proof do we have for this?"

Lev was stunned by this rather direct challenge. It was cunningly phrased and some heads nodded in agreement.

"How nice to meet you, Alfred. Your arguments sound plausible, I will admit. But no matter how much progress one has made in righteous living, this will not be the criteria for receiving everlasting life. No one has ever had a right to sin, even though they may have presumed so. The greatest work takes place in one's heart. The end of the commandment is love out of a pure heart. Let me ask you, can you be righteous and still come up short on love?"

Love for God Must Be Supreme

Alfred paused, somewhat taken aback. He then continued, "Your question seems a little unfair. If one is righteous, must it not follow that he loves righteousness?"

"I met our first parents when they returned. They were beautiful outwardly and inwardly. They were both righteous and without sin in the Garden of Eden. Mother Eve did not will to sin but was beguiled into sin. She was deceived. Why was she deceived? By her own admission, she disobeyed because she did not love the Lord with all her heart and strength and being. She would not have disobeyed if she had. You cannot love God supremely and disobey Him, can you?"

"I guess not," Alfred grudgingly admitted.

"It is not that our first parents did not love God. They did love God, but not enough to obey Him under the test conditions in which they found themselves. They failed on the very high plane of love in the heat of trial. By the way, I was their guide for awhile. I must tell you, they admitted they failed once, but they are quite determined not to fail the second time around! I doubt they will, because they are highly motivated to succeed in their devotion to God."

"How wonderful to hear that about our first parents, but how does that apply to us? We love God and our brothers and sisters. We cannot proclaim ourselves victors yet, but then neither are we already defeated before our final testing. Why do you wish us to feel guilty all the time? The more guilt we feel, the more we will work and sacrifice to offset our guilt. Is it guilt that drives people?"

Lev shook his head. "I certainly hope not. Remember the text, 'Though I give my body to be burned, and have not love, it profiteth me nothing' (1 Corinthians 13:3). Guilt does not atone for sin, nor does it count for righteousness. Where there is guilt, there is the reminder of sin that is not forgiven. Alfred, you know as well as I do that love must be the motivation behind all that we do. If we find ourselves doing less and less, it is certain that love is not motivating us. We know that God loves us, and He manifests that love by what He *has done* and *is doing* for us. I am certain that is God's view of our efforts as well. Love is not a passive emotion. It is known for what it does, for what it is willing to suffer and to endure."

Alfred paused to consider Lev's argument. "Okay. You have made your point very well, Lev. However, I still wonder. We have done all that was required and expected of us. We have not been remiss in caring for our loved ones and have even taken care of some we were not obligated to care for. So when are we free to enjoy a few moments for ourselves?"

"Alfred, you have always been free and will always be free to do whatever it is you wish to do. God has given each of us a free will. Our first parents were free to say 'no' to God, and they did. However, they were not free from the consequences of their choice, were they?"

"Maybe I am being a bit stubborn, Lev, but doesn't that make it seem as though God is interested in destroying good people, noble people, people that have exceeded what was required of them? The Christian religion once deteriorated into preaching that God was going to cast everyone that did not obey church dogmas into a burning hell. It gave the churches power over people, even though it was not true and clearly not biblical. Maybe Christ will love us for what we are—good and loving human beings—and not judge us for what we may have failed to do."

"Alfred," Lev replied softly. "Christ has an accurate knowledge of who are the 'sheep' that have tirelessly ministered to him and who are the 'goats' that have missed opportunities to do so. Nothing I say is going to change his assessment. You must realize that we are coming to the end of the thousand years. I do not know the exact date, and it has not been revealed. It is not important, therefore, for us to know the date, except the fact that there is going to be a separation of the 'sheep' from the 'goats.' 'Sheep' seem to be identified by what they did and 'goats' for what they failed to do. What more is there to say? Perhaps there is still time to change how the Master views our performance."

Facing the Issues

A troubled silence followed. Alfred realized his assessment was not holding up under tight scrutiny. Soon those assembled began to excuse themselves, thanking the host for a very stimulating evening. As Lev and Rebekah turned to leave, Ernest approached them.

"Please stay a moment. I would like to talk a little more about these matters. You have shed enough light on this subject so that I want to look at it more closely."

After all the guests had left except Lev, Rebekah and Ernest, they returned to the parlor for a face-to-face talk. Ernest continued, "I was very impressed with your reasoning in the discussion of this evening. I believe you are correct. My concern is, what should I do to make a difference? I realize I have lost some golden opportunities to serve my King. Is there time to remedy opportunities lost?"

"You certainly cannot change the past, Ernest. However, you can correct the present. I believe there is time to revise your position and become more active in serving our King." Lev knew that was true, because this was why the Ancients had sent them on their assignment. "Also, it is important that we assist others in looking for ways to serve our King. We all want to be an influence that inspires others in a more excellent way."

"I invited you to an upcoming concert, Lev, but perhaps I should cancel it and seek to find some service I can contribute toward serving the King. I know I have dismissed many opportunities, because I felt I had done my share. I realize now that was not the right thing to do. I feel a little like Scrooge on Christmas morning, who, having seen the past, present, and future, decided to change the future. If that is possible, that is what I shall try to do."

Naomi had listened throughout the evening and now joined the conversation. "Ernest has expressed my feelings exactly. I shared his smug feelings previously in passing off opportunities to serve our King, but suddenly I regret it. I am determined to renew my commitment to him. I do so appreciate our discussion this evening. It opened a window of insight that somehow had been closed and shuttered. Now light is streaming through it, for which I am so very grateful."

Rebekah responded sweetly. "It is so gratifying to hear your desire to change, Naomi. If you have decided to, then you will change. We can never do too much in the service of our King. We must remember what great things he has done for us."

"I understand exactly what you are saying. I am afraid my thinking was flawed for a season. Thank you! I am determined to make things right."

"If you are sincere in this matter," Lev added, "then it is important that you stand up and be counted. You know, we were sent by the Ancients because they feared an erroneous thought process was starting to develop here. You can help by speaking to others about your change of viewpoint. You may be able to help others also to change the future."

Ernest nodded in acknowledgment. "We have a great deal of influence in this community. Unfortunately, we have used it by encouraging others to place pleasure before duty. From now on, we are going to encourage our friends back into the service of our King."

"That is so encouraging to hear, Ernest! If we don't promptly obey the moment we recognize the need, it lessens the likelihood that we shall obey later. This is most gratifying to Rebekah and me. It indicates that a little encouragement in the right way might inspire the desire in others to change."

A Cloud Lifted

As they prepared to leave, Lev thanked Ernest and Naomi for the evening.

"I must confess, we came here hoping we could say something helpful. By the Lord's mercies, I believe we have succeeded. I hope you realize we sincerely enjoyed the music and poetry and your generous hospitality, but we enjoyed it under a cloud. Now that cloud has lifted. Thank you very much. As much as we will miss your concert this weekend, we know you have chosen greater service to our King."

"We then that are strong ought to bear the infirmities of the weak, and not to please ourselves"
(Romans 15:1).

Chapter Three

Lev and Rebekah were pleased to have had such quick success in the area of Basel. What a blessing to share the *true* joys of service in the regeneration work and not just the physical comforts! It was time to move on to another area that the Ancients had called to their attention—a place near former Zermatt in the Swiss Alps. The place where they were to land their small aircraft was in view of the majestic Matterhorn. Before landing they flew to the top of the mountain that overlooked Switzerland on one side and down into Italy on the other. It was breathtaking! People had struggled to scale this imposing height, and now without effort they hovered, absorbing the mountain grandeur in perfect comfort. Looking at the miniature villages below, life appeared so peaceful. Could there be anything but sweet contentment in such a beautiful setting?

All too soon, they landed along side of what was to be their home during their visit. The rustic Alpine lodge had many rooms for vacationers who traveled to view this picturesque area. Rebekah noticed the beautiful flower boxes brightly decorating every window. At one time the valley would have been filled with sheep and sheepherders, but now the animals wandered around at will. The protein grass on which they grazed was not only pleasing to the eye, but also nourishing. Along the back walls of the lodge, a large glass-enclosed area was filled with trees of life and other fruit trees, looking like a sculptured Garden of Eden. Everything was so charming, surely there would be no anxiety here concerning the ending of the thousand years or a loss of focus in serving the King.

"Welcome!" called Lisa, the lodge's hostess, as she led Lev and Rebekah to their rooms. She invited them for tea and lunch after they freshened up. Lisa managed the facility and lived in her own home down the road, serving as hostess several hours a day as her community service.

About twelve people sat around a large table with Lev and Rebekah. The mealtime discussion centered on the scenic view. During introductions, Lev was asked, "Was that your aircraft that hovered on top of the Matterhorn?"

"Yes," Lev laughed. "I decided to get to the top the easy way. It was worth it! We could see Italy and Switzerland in all their splendor."

A cheery, energetic man joined the conversation. "Greetings! I'm Zack, from Australia. I happened to be doing work in Switzerland and decided to take a day or two to visit here before leaving for home. Maybe you could give me a ride to the top of the Matterhorn? I would like that even better than climbing it!"

"Sure, Zack! Any time you want, just say the word. If there are others, we can take six at a time so everyone can take in the view from the top of the world," Lev replied enthusiastically.

Everyone at the table expressed their interest in the proposed adventure.

"Good. After lunch I'll take five passengers with me."

When Zack learned that Lev and Rebekah were from Israel and that they knew many of the Ancients personally, he asked the question for which they had been waiting.

"Say, since you have close contacts with Jerusalem, can either of you tell me when the thousand years will be ended? Back home in Australia that question comes up quite often. Lots of folks expect that it is very near. What do you think?"

No Inside Information

Lev responded, "Sorry, friend, we don't have any inside information."

"Well, somebody knows. Why is it such a secret?"

"It's not a secret to those who know. If such knowledge were necessary for us, I'm sure it would be revealed."

Zack looked somewhat taken aback. "No offense, Lev. I guess we are all curious. Knowing there is going to be a fixed time for Christ's reign to end, it is only logical to be interested in it. However, if it is not going to be revealed until after the fact, I have no problem with that. I haven't lost any sleep worrying about it. It was only a passing point of conversation on my part, really."

When everyone was finished eating, it came time to take the guests to the top of the Matterhorn. Lev took the first group and Rebekah waited with the second group until he returned.

After everyone was belted in, the aircraft lifted gently and easily. Lev explored all the features of the mountain as they ascended. When they reached the top, he flew to a vantage point where they could see both Italy and Switzerland. It was stunning, and all Lev could hear was "ooohs and "aahs." Even after centuries into the regeneration, no one ever tired of the loftiness of God's mountains, the vastness of His horizons, or the exaltation of the sky. They flew around for about twenty minutes at the top, gasping with delight at every new angle. Lev slowly brought the craft down, keeping close to see all the features of the mountain as they descended.

Everyone thanked him for such an exciting ride. Lev knew his guests would be pleased to hear, "Soon these aircraft will be more plentiful—everyone will have an opportunity to use them. The cost of building roads and bridges is avoided by supplying aircraft."

While Lev's group had been soaring on the mountaintop, Rebekah was sitting in front of a roaring fire chatting with Zoran and his friend Sebastian, while the rest of their lunch group listened with great interest. They had been sharing their philosophy that since everyone had been raised from the dead and great progress had been made toward perfection, it was time to sit back and enjoy life. They had been traveling around the world for the past six months, sightseeing and relaxing. Rebekah's side of the issue was that such thinking could potentially put them in danger of failing to achieve their ultimate goals of completely serving King Jesus. They were so engrossed in their conversation that no one even noticed that Lev had returned to take them for a ride.

Zoran was commenting, "You put too much significance on nonstop activity, Rebekah. When I look across the world, I see everyone rich, full, and satisfied. It is not as it was when we were bringing back four generations a year. That is when we had to work building homes, planting gardens, and keeping factories humming. Those years are long gone."

Lev listened quietly. He wondered how many in the group were agreeing with Zoran. Almost as if he had spoken his thoughts aloud, some of those who had been on the periphery of the discussion began adding their comments.

Working – A Joy

"I keep busy because I find opportunities to take on projects. If someone else wants to slack off, I don't mind. Everything seems to be getting done anyway."

"We enjoy helping—it's as natural as breathing to us. We don't know if we would be happier traveling and relaxing—that can get tiring."

"When you feel good, so full of energy, it is wonderful to be busy, especially in the King's business. I have had a week or two without any special work, and although I enjoyed my surroundings, I got fidgety. It isn't like when I had to work and felt weak, headachy, and tired. Why shouldn't we be productive?"

Zoran held his ground. "It seems to me that work ethics have had their drawbacks. People used to work day and night to get rich, yet when they became rich, they wanted more of everything. Then when they died, their children fought over the inheritance! Working for work's sake seems to be more of the same. We shroud it with altruism, but as we keep raising the standards of living higher, we have to work more—it becomes a vicious cycle. When is enough enough?"

Lev admitted that was clever logic, but he finally stepped into the discussion. "Well, Zoran, it seems to me that the work being done today isn't just adding more luxuries. If that were true, then you might have a good argument. But today we have what we need to eat, and no one is indulging in gluttony. Everyone has adequate housing, but no one is building himself or herself a mansion. Our goals now are not selfish. We are perfecting the tools of industry for higher standards of efficiency, taming the earth to prevent devastating earthquakes, and taming the atmosphere to prevent floods and vicious storms."

Rebekah added, "We have to break dams that caused imbalances in nature, clean up the environment from the toxic wastes, and be better managers of the earth. We have made tremendous progress, but we are not finished yet. We were commissioned to 'fill the earth and subdue it,' and until we have subdued it, we have work to do."

Sebastian listened carefully and finally said, "I guess maybe we have taken a rather short view of things. I didn't realize so much work was going on in all these fields. What you say is true. I have not seen anyone building huge mansions. Everyone seems more than satisfied with their existing homes and gardens."

The minutes were passing, and Lev had to remind them that another trip to the top of the Matterhorn was scheduled. "We are going to have to hurry if we want to go up today. Those clouds will be dropping on the mountain in less than a half hour. Of course, we could put it off until tomorrow."

"No, please," one of the guests said. "I am leaving tomorrow, and I really want to see the view from the top of the mountain."

"Okay, let's climb aboard! We'll make a quick trip of it."

A Call for Help

Just as everyone was seated and fastened in, an announcement came over the radio. "Attention, Lev Aron! Some people have climbed near the top of the Matterhorn and they see the clouds settling in. They are requesting that you pick them up before they get stranded. Over."

Lev replied, "Lev Aron, here. I see their location on the screen. How many are there? Over."

"Four. You must act quickly. Over"

"We're on our way. Over and out."

Lev unloaded everyone except the gentleman who was leaving the next day, asking him to stay to help. Soon they were airborne. Lev remembered seeing the ledge the climbers were on. It only took a minute to get there, but maneuvering the craft to hover in the right place with winds blowing was not going to be easy. Since the craft had enormous power and versatility, Lev kept it steady over the soon-to-be stranded climbers. No sooner were all four safely loaded and the door was shut, when the clouds started closing in on them. Lev knew they were just in time to safely fly back down.

"Thank you very much," exclaimed Lucas, a slight, freckled, blond who had been in charge of the climbing expedition. "It would have certainly been uncomfortable if we were to spend the night up there."

"Glad to help, Lucas!" Lev responded cheerfully. "How about some tea before you head on your way?"

"We are all staying at a house in the valley with landing pad 77. After we have some of your tea and warm ourselves by the fire, we would welcome a lift to our cabin."

Lisa brought in big mugs for everyone, while they warmed themselves at the fire. When they were cozily seated, Lucas brought up a question. "By the way, does anyone know if any progress is being made toward modifying the weather? I hear there has been some work on it. Is that really true?"

Lev responded, "Yes, Lucas, I happened to be working on one of those projects. We were able to modify certain weather patterns, but more work is needed to do this on the kind of scale that you are talking about. Mountains of this size create all kinds of weather abnormalities. I think in the next few years we will see real progress in some procedures that should be very effective in taming the weather."

He continued as everyone gave his or her undivided attention. "I was working with a task force in Japan not long ago. Different groups were working on the same problem in other nations. When we compared our research, we found one solution that really appeared to be effective, only we did not have the equipment yet that was powerful enough to affect large areas."

Why Did You Stop?

Lucas was curious. "If I had some training in that field, I would volunteer in a heartbeat. However, by the time I got into it, they would have it solved I suppose."

Zoran, who had been relaxing the past hour or so in a cozy chair at the side of the fireplace, was taking in this exchange. He finally turned to Lev and said, "You know what? I think I have been wrong. Listening to you folks talk, I realize that you have been working for the common good of mankind, while I have been spending time just doing nothing but seeking my own comfort and pleasure. Lev, you, Rebekah, and Lucas convinced me. I am done sitting on my hands. Can you suggest anything I can do in the service of our King?"

"Yes," Lev said. "While you are here, you and all who share your renewed enthusiasm can spread the word. We do have a confession to make. Rebekah and I were sent here by the Ancients because of their concern that some might be losing the vision of service to our King."

"Oh, my!" Sebastian gasped. "That does it for me! Obviously we have been fooling ourselves. There is nothing to stop us from enjoying life while working for the common good. I do not understand how mixed up one can be. I certainly can see it all now!" He turned to Zoran with a smile. "Zoran, our vacation ends today! Starting tomorrow, it's back into joyful service! What do you say?"

"Absolutely!"

Lucas chimed in, "Count me in also. I think I would rather be doing something constructive than freezing out on the Matterhorn anyway."

A cheer went up from the whole group.

Lucas said, "I think this meeting was providential, Lev. We not only were spared a nasty night on the mountain, but we learned we have been drifting away from the service of our King. Thanks again, friends! That was the best thing that happened to us today."

An Evening by the Fire

The evening weather turned foul, and everyone was happy to stay around the large fireplace, sipping tea and fellowshipping. The congenial group, having learned that Lev and Rebekah were very familiar with the Ancients, had a number of questions.

Many were curious to know how the Ancients lived. They had seen them on television and on many of the teaching programs, but they knew rather little of their personal lives. Tania, a botanist from West Africa, asked, "Tell us about the Ancients. They do not seem to mix much with the rest of the people. Is that because they are so busy?"

Rebekah answered, "They are busier than you can imagine. Because the world's time varies twenty-four hours, there is never a time the Ancients cannot be reached. They are entirely dedicated to the service of Christ. They keep track of everything going on in the world, are on top of all scientific endeavors, and know how to pull together the most gifted minds to solve problems. In addition, they deal with many serious personal problems. When people were still being punished for misdeeds, they handled every case. As if all this were not enough, they are concerned with individuals who are not responding as they should. At present, too many people are ceasing to prioritize their activities to give themselves in needful service."

"How do they live?" another woman asked. "Do they have palatial dwellings with many servants?"

Rebekah answered, "You would be very surprised. They are living in the Old City of Jerusalem. Many of the buildings are quite old and not very impressive to look at. I don't mean that they are shabby. After all, all they would need to do is ask, and the workers would build them palaces to live in. But they only request that these buildings be kept clean and sturdy. They eat as you and I do, often with very short breaks for lunch and supper. When they are not working, they are resting. However, when you meet them, their wonderful spirit is an inspiration. We are so blessed to have such gifted, faithful and loving servants. For all these centuries they have served freely and without compensation of any kind."

Lev joined in, "You have to see them in their work and home setting to appreciate their dedicated lifestyle. There is no show or ostentation in anything they do. Rebekah and I have been privileged to meet with them many times over the centuries, but never have they been unkind or even short with us. In the early days everything was rather chaotic in the world. The transition from the old world into the new way of doing things took enormous patience and effort on their part. Now everything is reasonably stable. How they ever managed to keep their hands on everything during that critical transition time is a miracle."

Tania asked, "You are leaving out one part of the story. Isn't the secret to their success that they have contact with Christ and his body members?"

"I am glad you mentioned that, Tania," Lev responded, "Yes, that is the secret to their loving and caring service for mankind. They are privy to information that you and I are not. One cannot differ with the Ancients without differing with Christ."

Who Can Replace the Ancients?

Tania pursued her questioning. "What's going to happen when the Ancients step out of office? How are we ever going to get along without them?"

Rebekah nodded, "I wish everyone had the appreciation you have toward our leaders. I am sure there are many who once had authority that would like to have it again. Given the fact that the pages of history were darkened by an endless succession of people who managed to sit in authority over others, I would not be surprised to see a host of ungrateful people demanding that the Ancients step out of office when the thousand years are ended."

Tania was appalled. "Oh, how awful! How could anyone even think of that?"

"Tania, you are a person after my own heart," Lev said. "Already I have encountered people wondering when the thousand years are going to be officially ended. Some are beginning to worry that the Ancients may overstay their allotted time in office, even though that is the last thing in the world anyone should be concerned about. They ought to be watching their own hearts instead."

Rebekah added. "The real issue now is the separation of the 'sheep' from the 'goats.' Just because people are careful to avoid sin, it is easy to think that will be sufficient to gain Christ's approval. But there is more required — we must manifest a heart filled with love for God and our fellow men."

"Shall he that contendeth with the Almighty instruct Him?"
(Job 40:2)

Chapter Four

The community near the Matterhorn had retained its quaintness and charm. The setting was enchanting with pure and fresh air. Unmoved by time, by storms, and even by man's presence, the mountain towering in the distance spoke of God's sovereignty and testified to His glory. Since there was soon to be an annual festival where villagers and visitors would enjoy a day of fellowship, Lev and Rebekah decided to remain at the lodge until then.

The production of personal aircraft was finally catching up to the needs of various areas, and this particular weekend the town would be receiving ten new ones similar to Lev's. Lev and Rebekah were asked to instruct the people on operating the vehicles safely. Though the aircraft would not be assigned to individuals, people would be free to use them as needed. This community fleet would reduce the need for roads, enable people and supplies to be transported easily, and assist animals or people stranded by the elements. Excitement permeated the air.

While waiting for the arrival of the new aircraft, Lev and Rebekah gave flying lessons. Although the craft was stable and easy to manage, training was needed for every possible situation they might encounter. The fact that people could be taught their use before the new aircraft arrived was a real benefit. Quite a number received thorough training, even though none had taken a solo flight yet. Everyone wanted to take the aircraft to the top of the Matterhorn to see the divide.

The plan was to train twenty people, who would later teach others. Ultimately, everyone in the community would be instructed to operate the aircraft and enjoy their efficiency and comfort.

A Difficulty Arises

Training classes went very smoothly because people were intelligent, capable and eager. Once they learned something, their minds retained it. Difficulties arose when some wanted to use the aircraft for visiting the Matterhorn for pleasure and curiosity rather than necessity. The aircraft were to be used freely to improve transportation and to ferry visitors from the airport who desired to see the Matterhorn, not for personal travel. Larger airplanes were to be used for long-distance travel.

During these sessions, Lev and Rebekah had an opportunity to get acquainted with many of the villagers, enabling them to focus on their current assignment. They found some were truly concerned that they may not have been as faithful as they could have been, while others were quite confident that they would be approved during the final testing.

What was intended to be a strong community benefit was soon becoming a community problem. Lev had trained Hans Nielsen to fly until he successfully soloed. Hans was gifted in his ability to fly, but he was also quick to understand how the apparatus functioned and how to maintain it properly. Lev felt that Hans would make an excellent choice to service these aircraft. However, Hans spoke freely to Lev of his desire to see the world in one of these new machines. At first, Lev thought Hans was just carried away with the excitement of learning to fly, but he soon learned Hans was entirely serious.

Finally, Lev said, "You know, Hans, these aircraft are not provided for anyone to use for personal pleasure. They are community service machines. Anyone who needs them should not be deprived because one is not available due to abuse of the arrangements."

Hans retorted, "I see you and Rebekah have an aircraft for your own private pleasure. Why am I different?"

"I am afraid you are mistaken, Hans. We are here on assignment from the Ancients. In addition to teaching the proper use of the aircraft, we have been asked to encourage people who, while living on a high moral plane and conducting themselves within the law, are seeking pleasure over serving their fellow man."

"You can't be serious, Lev! Have you forgotten the progress people have made from their former life? Some were murderers, others thieves, and the list could go on and on. Now they are living well within the limits of righteousness. There would be no reason whatever to destroy good people. No, I can't believe that."

Lev sighed. It was painful to deliver a rebuke, but this was a life-and-death issue. "Hans, if you would restudy the Parable of the Sheep and the Goats, you might be surprised what information it contains."

"I assumed that if the 'goats' are destroyed, they must be bad people. Most people I know are good people. I don't see how good people will be in any danger. That's not possible."

"What is your definition of good, Hans?"

"I used to be a bad person. I lied a lot. I abused people and was actually a thief. I think I know what a bad person is like. Now, I am completely reformed. I wouldn't even be tempted to steal anything or to deceive anyone. Are you telling me I may not be good enough?"

"No, I am not your judge. I try not to judge myself or anyone else. But if you read the Parable of the Sheep and Goats carefully, you will notice that the two classes are separated rather uniquely. The 'sheep' are commended for having actively ministered to Christ, while the 'goats' are condemned for their failure to serve the King in little hidden ways that demonstrated their lack of love."

Serving the Needs of Others

Hans nodded his head. "Now that you mention it, I see your point. What you are telling me, Lev, is that if I were to take this aircraft just to explore the area for pleasure, I would not be serving the interests of others and, therefore, I would not be serving the King."

Lev was amazed how quickly sound reasoning was absorbed by those whose heart conditions were prepared to receive wise counsel. "Thank you for that hidden insight. I promise that I will repair these aircraft faithfully and only use them in serving the needs of my brothers and sisters. I guess I was acting like a 'goat,' wasn't I?"

Lev smiled at Hans's humility. "It is not up to me to label the 'sheep' or the 'goats.' I only know it is important to keep yourself available to serve our King wherever and whenever needed, Hans."

"I don't *think* that I have shirked my duties, Lev. I built houses for all of my family and relatives and even some people I didn't know. I don't think I have passed up anyone who was hungry or in need."

"I know what you are saying, Hans, but in the parable the 'goats' were quite surprised with Christ's assessment of them and were quick to defend their position. They even insisted that they had been diligent in Christ's service."

"Do you think, Lev, that I might be too late now and that I am already marked as a 'goat'?"

"Oh no, Hans," Lev quickly assured. "Apparently there is still time, though not much, to please our King. God and Christ do not desire that any should perish."

"Lev, I thank you for talking to me so frankly. I may have developed a philosophy that made me feel more confident than I should. I think some of my friends may have drawn some of the same conclusions. We have been flattering each other with false assurances."

"Why don't you bring them to where I am staying? I would love to meet them and talk to them. The Ancients *are* worried about people who are putting themselves in danger without even realizing it. The main problem is that many appear to be good and decent people since they have lived this long. But it is possible to act correctly outwardly, but not be right in one's heart, which is what is needed to pass the test. There is cause for concern."

"I have two friends who want to learn to fly these aircraft, and I promised to teach them. We will stop at the lodge where you are staying tomorrow night after they get done with their work at the local factory. Would that be okay with you?"

"Sounds good to me, Hans—I hope we can help them take a better view of their privileges."

A Disappointing Meeting

Hans arrived early the following evening with his two friends, Tobias and Jacques. They understood that Lev had been instrumental in building the aircraft, and they were impressed with that, but they seemed a bit uncomfortable. Obviously, Hans had told them the main purpose of the Arons' trip to the area.

The young men wanted to know all about the internal secrets of the aircraft and what problems had to be solved to bring it into mass production. While they examined all the mechanical features of the vehicle, they questioned Lev extensively to gain as much knowledge as possible. Lev answered all their queries thoroughly and with great expertise. However, when Lev turned the subject around to personal responsibilities, both Tobias and Jacques became visibly ill at ease.

When Lev affirmed his real reason for being in the area, Tobias said, "You sure know your stuff about this aircraft, Lev, but you seem to be unhappy to see people having a good time. What is the point, unless you enjoy life to its fullest?"

"Yeah," Jacques echoed sullenly. "I've heard that unless a person is standing on his head being miserable doing a job for someone that ought to be doing the job himself, you become irritated, Lev."

Tobias spoke confidently, "We did more than our share of work and it's time for other people to pull their own load."

"That's exactly right," Jacques agreed. "We feel we're being assaulted with a line of reasoning calculated to make us feel guilty. Why can't we accept that Utopia is here and begin to enjoy it? Why are you spreading fear of annihilation, because we aren't accepting the work people should do for themselves?"

"That's what I say!" Tobias excitedly exclaimed. "Everybody's needs are supplied generously, so why is there still work to be done? We have worked rigorously in this regenerating program. It was a good work. We believed in it, and it was fairly carried out. We have no complaints about that. Never has the world had such efficiency, nor has mankind been lifted to so high a state of development. But isn't it enough already?"

Lev listened attentively, taken aback by the aggressive stand of his two guests. "If that is what you have decided, you have that right. However, it is my responsibility to tell you that such relaxation may not last very long for you. Whether you realize it or not, this splendid age was not only intended to accomplish the regeneration of the human race, but it must also accomplish something even harder. And that is putting love in the human heart to replace selfishness. Unless this is attained, Christ will not continue anyone's existence past the end of the thousand years."

Lev's answer did not satisfy Jacques. "Some think the thousand years may be ended already. If that's so, we're still here and your ministry of fear is nothing but a false cry of 'wolf.' Anyway, even the wolf is tame now. So why are you still in a frenzy about carrying on projects that have no assigned time limits?"

Lev could see the two men were absolutely convinced of their position. So he rested his usual arguments and said, "I see that these are apparently your deeply-held convictions. May I ask if you are content to believe these things yourself, or are you trying to convince others?"

Standing for Convictions

Tobias replied, "Once you're convinced of something, integrity requires that you stand up and be counted for your beliefs. How could we be wrong though? We're not advocating evil of any kind, nor do we sympathize with it. We're good people with high ideals. We've labored and accomplished more than our fair share."

Lev only shook his head sadly. "If you base your conclusions on justice alone, I see how you can come to your conclusions. Doesn't love require more than mere justice? Justice simply demands you weigh out exactly the right amount and no more. Love requires that you give more, heaping it up and spilling it over. Could it be that the test being visited upon us now is to see who is governed by strict justice, and who not only meets justice, but generously exceeds it in love?"

Jacques stiffly replied, "There you go, Lev, never satisfied. For those of us who were once sinners and never concerned too much with justice, we've come a long way. We've gone beyond justice too. We labored to help many people to whom we owed nothing from the past life. You're judging us without a fair reading."

"Listen, Jacques," Lev said, "I am not your judge or even a part of the jury. I am not sure that Christ is going to accept your thinking, though. However, you are free to believe what you want. I can only wish you the best. However, I think your reasoning is seriously flawed. And I am worried to see you advocating it to others."

Tobias wryly commented, "Don't worry about that. We're not as smooth a talker as you are, Lev. And we don't have a following, if that is what you are implying. We're just not going to have a guilt trip laid upon us. We are good people. That doesn't seem to matter to you, and I think it should."

"I appreciate your claims of loyalty to the King. I hope I have that kind of loyalty to him, too. However, your whole analysis is failing in one important point. The sins of omission are what seal the doom of the 'goat' class. At least that is how I read the parable of Matthew 25. Maybe I am wrong, but I don't think so. Read it over again."

Jacques answered defensively, "You seem determined to leave us feeling guilty. Obviously, you seem to be implying that we may be the 'goats.' Why don't you give us some encouraging words instead of all these insinuations?"

"I am sorry if I have been burdensome." Lev had no desire just to cause pain, but his love for humanity pushed him forward. "You must understand that I was sent into this area because the Ancients felt there was a need to encourage the same spirit of giving and sacrifice with which so many started out. Now it seems to have been lost. Perhaps *attitude* should be part of this discussion. If it is a burden to do a little extra for the common good, then we won't have a good time doing it. On the other hand, if we delight to do the little extra things from our hearts, we will enjoy it greatly."

A Good Listener

Hans sat through this whole discussion listening carefully to the reasons on both sides. As they were about to leave, he said, "I have been silent during this whole discussion. I am sorry I have to disagree with you, Tobias and Jacques. You both have been my steadfast friends for a long time. I think I had come under your way of thinking, but now I am determined to make a straight path for my feet. We cannot love too much or be too generous. If I am going to err, it is going to be on the side of an uninhibited giving of myself in the service of others."

Tobias laughed and said, "You'll still be our friend, Hans. Lev has given you unnecessary guilt. Just train us on these aircraft."

Lev answered, "I am not trying to make anyone feel guilty. Simply consider rationally what is your true position before your King."

Jacques said, "Hans may be smarter than we are, Tobias. I was absolutely sold on my position as I entered into this discussion, but Lev pricked my conscience a bit. We're strong and healthy with enormous energy. Why not use it constructively?"

"Oh, no, Jacques! You're not accepting guilt, too, are you? Can't you see this is the same old trick they used to use on us? Remember the better-be-good sermons the churches laid on people? 'If you don't repent, you'll go to hell and burn forever.' Now where are the fires of hell? Most of those who preached falsehoods like these don't even want to be reminded of their sermons."

"Yes, Tobias," Lev contended. "You are absolutely right about what happened in the past. But that is an unfortunate comparison to make. The warning of danger is not coming from misguided teachers today. It is coming from the Ancients. They have not made any mistakes in this whole regeneration process. Do you think that they are making a mistake now? I know you think you are good and that good people could not possibly come to grief. Remember, our first parents were good—however, under the test they failed to show that they loved the Lord their God supremely."

Tobias turned a little red. "I don't know if I'm being stubborn or foolish, but I guess the idea that we are being tested irritates me. Why is it that being good may not be enough? That makes me feel that all of my growth and development to be a righteous and honorable human being counts for nothing, if I am not in perpetual motion doing some good work somewhere for someone. Is it just me that is having a problem here, or are there others?"

The Test Is Character

Lev responded delicately. "Many Christians once believed that all they had to do was accept Jesus and that would guarantee them entrance to heaven. Yet most of them are still right here on earth. They were good people, but they failed to see that eternal life cannot be given to anyone just for identifying with Jesus. Professing our Savior is not enough. We need to develop a character likeness to that of the Master. That is what this is all about. Character, *character*, <u>*character*</u>."

Tobias spoke again. "I tell you, I *am* a good person! I can't believe that anyone who conducts himself righteously is going to be lost!"

Lev replied, "Tobias, if you were going to give eternal life to anyone, how concerned would you be about his or her character?"

"I suppose I would be concerned that such a person had demonstrated a remarkable degree of kindness."

"Would you be satisfied with someone who has just kept on the right side of the law?"

Tobias was obviously shaken by this line of reasoning. "I don't know about those who live at the border of righteousness. I wouldn't know if there was any danger that they might stray over the line. Certainly, I wouldn't want to grant eternal life to anyone who was not absolutely committed to righteousness. One experiment with sin has been *enough*. I guess I would be very reticent to grant eternal life to anyone whom I might doubt."

"Tobias, you have stated the case accurately. Those who gain everlasting life must be people whose lives demonstrate they love righteousness and hate iniquity. The only way you can prove that is to measure their love for God's laws and for their fellow men, not by just one test, but by the way they conduct themselves when no one is looking day after day, and year after year. Those who are extravagant in giving themselves to others are better choices for eternal life than those who squeak by with the least they can do. Wouldn't you agree?"

"Yes, you are right, Lev. I confess that I was looking at matters from my own point of view. I must admit I would rather see people destroyed in the second death than to see sin become active in this world again. One experience with sin is enough. I appreciate the fact that God is not going to allow sin to be active in this world ever again."

Hans hugged Tobias and shouted, "Hooray! Lev, you now have three converts who are committed to living by the law of love for others!"

"And the work of righteousness shall be peace; and the effect of righteousness quietness and assurance for ever" (Isaiah 32:17).

Chapter Five

A flutter of e-mails had come in to the Ancients requesting that they address the issue of the end of the reign of Christ. Questions included: "Why aren't you clarifying matters?" "If you know, why don't you tell us?" "Why not end all discussion with a plain statement of the truth?" Some individuals even contributed their studies on the subject and suggested possible termination points of the reign.

Everyone knew that Christ, the Mediator, would cease to represent the people before God at some point. They knew that the approximate time for the separation of the 'sheep' from the 'goats' would soon take place.

The Ancients called Lev and Rebekah back to Jerusalem. They had a new and unusual task for them. The Arons entered the conference room finding the usual warm greetings and loving exchanges from the Worthies who were to meet with them that day. John the Baptist, the cousin of Jesus and the last Ancient Worthy to have lived, wasted no time getting to the point.

"Lev and Rebekah, thank you for coming. Some of our brothers and sisters require direction in this matter of when the reign of Christ will end and when the separation of the 'sheep' and 'goats' will take place. As you probably realize, we cannot reveal any specific information respecting this test. Though the entire matter is in the hands of Christ, people think we owe them information because they simply want their curiosity satisfied.

We are forbidden to provide such information, because it is not relevant to the overall good of mankind. Of course, we cannot tell you either. However, there is a lot of information that you *can* know. What we want you to do is to go on television. We will allow people to call in their questions on the air. We would like you to answer them, not with specific information, but with reason and candor. They need to know that these questions, while logical, are not appropriate to ask."

Rebekah quickly responded, "You know we are willing to take any assignment, but you may want to cue us on appropriate answers. We have done the best we could on our assignments, and with some success, but on the screen it might be harder."

"Just remember that you are on the airwaves to tell them to go about life with love in their hearts and an eagerness to be helpful to others," Moses suggested. "Answering specific questions about details of time will not have any relevance in revealing who are the 'sheep' and who are the 'goats.' If the answers would make a difference, then it would be unfair not to reveal this knowledge. But since time and dates will not affect character, they will not be told."

"Why is this matter starting to come up now?" Rebekah asked.

"Because people are nervous as the end of this age approaches," Sarah replied. "Some are worried that they may be 'goats' or that some of their special friends may be. It is only natural to try to look into the future. Everyone knows Satan is going to be loosed, but there will be some confusion as to whether he is released or not. That will be one aspect of the test."

Joseph continued, "Will we challenge Satan's deception? We could expose his deception rather easily, but we won't. It is all a part of the testing process. Those whose hearts are right will never be in danger of being deceived. Those who are eager to believe a lie will have an opportunity to do so. These tests are necessary, because only those who love the Lord our God with all their heart and mind and being are going to be rewarded with everlasting life."

The Image of God

"Everyone has been given the most wonderful opportunities to regain the image of God in their hearts," Huldah explained. "Most have availed themselves of this opportunity in a magnificent way. Others failed early on and were destroyed. Some have become righteous, but they are still lacking in fervent love for God and their fellow men. Satan is a skillful deceiver and has had a long time in the abyss to sharpen his wits. However, God is going to use Satan as He did in the Garden of Eden, permitting him to mislead any who are sympathetic to his deceptions. It is vitally important that only the righteous and loving in heart be granted eternal life. Those with impure hearts would never be truly happy under God's regime of justice and love."

Rebekah was still puzzled. "Wouldn't it be better to have one of your own impressive members handle the inquiries? The Ancients are a respected community of leaders. What people really want is a direct response from you. It is always better to get your answers from the top, rather than from some lesser source. What kind of credentials do we have that anyone would acknowledge us?"

John the Baptist quickly acknowledged her point. "You have touched a very sensitive issue, Rebekah. You are quite correct in your assessment. If we took to the airwaves to answer their questions, it would have more weight. On the other hand, because we all know more than we are allowed to tell, our absolute knowledge and honesty might enable some to deduce the approximate truth if we answered enough questions. You may truthfully tell them that you do not know, and then proceed to deal with their questions, not from the standpoint of absolute knowledge, but from the standpoint of honesty and healthy reasoning. That should convince people that this information is not available to them, because it will have no bearing on anyone's performance. What people do under very relaxed conditions is going to determine whether they are 'sheep' or 'goats.' What is done from the heart when no one is looking or taking notice is what is going to count."

Lev agreed, "I see your point exactly. You are being flooded with requests for knowledge that is not to be revealed to everyone yet."

"Right, Lev. We are authorizing you to answer inquiries without absolute knowledge," advised Elijah. "If we were to tell you, then we might as well get on the air ourselves. Since we are forbidden from making the information known, there is no use telling the people we know the answers, but we will not tell them. It would not be kind. But you can tell them honestly that you do not know, and then point out that this information has not been provided by Christ and, therefore, it is not proper to ask."

"Your point is well taken," Rebekah nodded. "Can we tell them what we do know? Can we tell them that we are near the end of the reign of Christ and there still may be time to show their love for God and our fellow men? Some want to know why Satan is to be loosed out of his prison. What shall we tell them? Is there still another test upon mankind even after the 'sheep' and 'goats' are separated?"

Released to Deceive

"Of course you may tell them what you know, Rebekah," John the Baptist answered. "The reason Satan is being loosed from his prison is plainly stated to 'deceive the nations' (Revelation 20:8). Yes, there will be another test after the 'sheep' and 'goats' are separated. You may also tell them that only those who have their names in the 'Lamb's book of life' (Revelation 21:27), will become citizens of the 'New Jerusalem.'"

Sarah added, "This is a critical time because the Lord is going to manifest what is really in the hearts of people. Some may pass one test and fail another. However, no one will fail who loves God supremely and his neighbor as himself."

Then John the Baptist provided further details. "If you accept this mission, Lev and Rebekah, we will put you on after the early evening report on the news and progress that we provide each evening. We will announce that your program will deal with open questions at the end of our next two broadcasts. You will have two days to prepare and to pray about your answers. The program will be a half-hour session to answer questions we receive after our announcement. Our aides will help you categorize groups of questions. This way the flood of inquiries can all be addressed. However, we want you to deal with people's feelings and anxieties, both for themselves and their loved ones. We do not want anyone to come away feeling put down and demeaned for asking their questions. If people won't respond to love, they won't respond to anything."

"Thank you for the opportunity to help," Lev responded solemnly. "Not that we feel especially capable, but we leave that to your judgment. If you want us, you have us."

"We thank you, Lev and Rebekah," Sarah responded. "People don't want to be locked out of information that is available. Perhaps when they learn that no announcement will be made about when the thousand years are ended, it will quell the tide of questions. The program will not be long. When people learn certain things are not revealed and are not going to be, most of them will be satisfied."

"I am glad we will have a little time to prepare for this. If we need help, may we call on you?" Rebekah inquired.

"Certainly, Rebekah!" Sarah answered.

Elijah added, "Curiosity as to when the thousand years will end is normal and innocent. Just as there have been various stages in Christ's reign, so this leaves the matter of the ending with some uncertainty. This was not an oversight. Knowing when Christ's reign ends will have no bearing on anyone's ultimate achievement. Everyone has known that this has been a time of probation to demonstrate what is within his or her heart. Some think that just living a pure and sinless life guarantees them a place in the Lamb's Book of Life. They must realize that sins of omission are also an index of the heart."

When Told to Exit Office, We Will

"When the thousand years are ended," John the Baptist continued, "people are going to want to know about us. How long will we be in power? When will earth's rule be placed back in the hands of the general public? This may raise some serious concerns. The moment Christ tells us to step out of office, we will. Until then, we will stay in power regardless of when Christ's reign ends. There will be further tests after the 'sheep' and 'goats' are separated. The time before us is going to reveal those who love God above all and those who fail to love God supremely. It is a very serious time."

The meeting ended with a prayer by Moses. Lev and Rebekah thanked the Ancients for the privilege of serving their King in this new capacity, even though they left the room feeling rather nervous. Trying to allay people's concerns was a difficult assignment.

The First Program

By the time the first evening for this special program arrived, Lev and Rebekah had received literally thousands of questions, but with the help of the staff, they were able to organize the questions into categories. Settling into their chairs, they smiled into the cameras showing a confidence they didn't feel.

The first question was quite blunt. "When will the thousand years of Christ's reign end?"

Lev started, "I have no knowledge about the precise date. We know that we are close. Christ knows the date and you may be sure he will not reign longer than he is supposed to. Other than to satisfy curiosity, how does it advantage us to know any date?"

The next question was directed to Rebekah. "When will Satan be loosed?"

She answered, "Satan will be loosed when the thousand years are ended. That much is clearly stated in the Bible. I think the questioners want to know the day and hour of Satan's release, and only Christ knows that. Any answer as to the precise time has not been provided to us. If the questioner wishes to know why this information is being withheld, that is another matter. Knowing a particular point of time for his release is not an important factor in our reactions to his deceptions. It should not be difficult for those who love God supremely. We have been protected from lies all during Christ's reign. If Satan is permitted to deceive, it only means that there are those among us who are willing to be deceived."

The next question was directed to Lev. "If the 'goats' are destroyed because of sins of omission, does this mean that salvation is by works after all?"

"Salvation has been made possible by Christ. Only Christ has provided the means for us to move upward to regain the image of God in our hearts. Ministering to those in need requires effort and sacrifice, but it has never been an oppressive service. There is a certain degree of reward in just helping others. If opportunities to serve are repeatedly refused, it may indicate a lack of love for our fellow men and also for Christ, who is affording us these opportunities."

Rebekah was given the next question. "Are there two different ways that people are going to fail to gain eternal life? One by sins of omission as the 'goats' are accused of, and the other, those that engage in a sin of commission as those who join in Satan's deception?

Good—Not Good Enough

"That is what the Bible teaches. People have lived throughout this period of Christ's reign, and to come to the end of his reign means that they have made a great deal of progress. At this point in time everyone lives righteously. So they have all learned to live by very high standards. But what must be demonstrated is whether they are good enough. The 'goats' obviously did not do more than they were required to do and will lose Christ's commendation. He observes a lack in their character. They were good enough to keep from doing evil, but not vigilant in selfless love. However, some may have been diligent in serving others yet carry a hidden sympathy for sin in their hearts. Perhaps they had thoughts like, 'If it were permitted, I would do such and such. But since it is not permitted, I can't.' When Satan is heard from again, these will find a degree of sympathy with his message. His deception will be subtle, but only hearts that do not love God supremely will respond to him. So, yes, there are two different tests that will eliminate those who do not have perfect love."

The broadcasts had been listened to eagerly and gave Lev and Rebekah worldwide recognition as servants of the Ancients. The fact that they were used instead of one of the Ancients raised a lot of eyebrows, because the Ancients were the official agents of Christ. Why were people of lesser stature used? People were mentally perfect and did not miss making astute observations. Chief of the conjectures that resulted from this was, could it be that the Ancients were about to step out of office?

People were sensing that the end of an age was soon to take place and started thinking seriously. Just as young people never worried about old age, so people during this long period of peace and restoration never gave much thought as to how the era would end. The final test had seemed far away—things were going so well, surely they would continue the same way.

Deception to Be Possible Again

But suddenly time had passed. The thought of separation between the "sheep" and "goats" began to be worrisome. Realizing that Satan would soon be loosed out of his prison was disturbing. New freedoms being permitted by Satan created an alarm that deception was a real possibility, even though most people were sure they would not be deceived. They were too smart for this now. After the Arons' broadcast, people began to speak openly. Everyone was alerted to the fact that the age would end with serious consequences for those not imbued with God's Spirit.

*"Trust in the Lord with all thine heart;
and lean not unto thine own understanding"
(Proverbs 3:5).*

Chapter Six

Everywhere Lev went in public he was recognized from the TV programs he had been on. People felt free to approach him and ask about statements that he had made on TV or to openly express a differing view. He did not mind at first, but soon he found himself being engaged in endless discussions. He found it was better to listen to these people and thank them for their point of view. On a few occasions he was challenged to debate issues. He graciously declined saying, "If I am asked by the Ancients to debate I will gladly do so, but to do so without authorization would be inappropriate."

One afternoon, Lev was in the garden selecting some vegetables for his dinner when a neighbor strolled over for a casual visit. Liam was a muscular man with a gentle demeanor. He and Lev had enjoyed many evenings of study and conversation through the years. During the course of their fellowship, Liam asked, "After the Ancients step out of office, who will lead us?"

"Well, Liam, let's wait on the Lord until then. If we wait long enough, the answer to all of these questions will be known and no further discussion will be necessary."

"I don't doubt that Christ has the knowledge, but he certainly has not shown a desire to share it with us. Without absolute knowledge are we not free to think and speak about such things to enlarge our understanding of matters?"

"We can only go so far," Lev replied. "After that it becomes an unprofitable exercise. We have lived for centuries without knowing. Why has it suddenly become a burning issue? We only know for sure what is clearly written in God's Word, after that we should tread lightly."

Liam simply shrugged his shoulders, then chuckled and said, "Lev, you are a hard man to debate with. Have a nice dinner. Shalom."

Lev was glad to find himself home for a season, more or less out of public view. Rebekah was having similar experiences, and they both were glad to settle quietly into community life for a while.

Lev learned that his former father-in-law had also recently returned home now that most of his work was completed. Rebekah asked to join Lev when he went to spend a day with her parents. When they landed on Benjamin Obadiah's pad, he ran out to eagerly welcome them. After hugs and greetings they went to sit in his beautiful garden. Soon Deborah, Rebekah's mother, joined them. She had been expecting them and spotted their craft.

Deborah exclaimed, "We're so glad to see you! It seems we are never home at the same time. But the big push for the trees of life is over, so we have come back to our plants that seem glad to have us home again."

"Mother, I can believe that!" Rebekah remarked. "I often thought your plants would wither if you did not speak to them." Everyone laughed at that comment.

They shared the pleasure of one another's company around the kitchen table, catching up on their personal experiences.

"You can't imagine how often we're asked how we will know when the thousand years are ended and Satan is loosed," Rebekah shook her head.

"That is the perennial question. We don't have to know the day or the hour to be aware of his devices. We do know some things, however," said Benjamin. "The separation of the 'sheep' from the 'goats' precedes Satan's loosing. You can see the difference between 'sheep' and 'goats.' Our Lord is referred to as the 'Lamb' in Revelation over twenty-five times and a 'lion' once. It is the 'Lamb' who overcomes all foes and brings in righteousness. The qualities of the 'Lamb' are represented in Christ and all who have learned of him."

"That's right," replied Lev. "And 'goats' are more pleasure-loving and like the high places. They aren't savage creatures, but they're not as docile as lambs and are more independent. That tells us why the 'goats' are judged unfavorably and go into 'eternal punishment' of death at the end of Christ's reign."

Benjamin explained further, "The fact that the 'goats' were kept alive until the end of Christ's reign shows us that they could be kept alive indefinitely if Christ wanted it that way. However, eternal life is reserved only for those who love God as Jesus did—that is, supremely. Still, there remains one more test after this. Some may have looked like 'sheep' and acted like them as well. However, they are rebels just waiting for a leader and a cause to step forward into action."

"So, then, the thousand years will end after the 'sheep' and 'goats' are separated," Rebekah observed.

"That's how it would seem to me," Benjamin nodded.

"And this will signal the time of Satan's release from his confinement, not the day and hour, but it should put everyone on alert that the old deceiver may be at work starting to sow his seeds of deception," Lev interjected.

"I think so," Benjamin responded. "Those who wait upon the Lord can wait patiently for the Lord to make His will known. They don't have to join every frenzied cry for change or try to take matters into their hands. Christ ran everything perfectly during his reign, so why not wait to see what he will bring to pass in his good pleasure at his due time."

A Wiley Foe

A canary landed on Rebekah's shoulder, and she stroked its head for a moment.

"I am sure that many ideas will be advanced that will seem logical. Satan is a wily foe and very subtle. He implied that the tree of knowledge would bring knowledge to Eve that God was withholding from her unnecessarily. He implied the fruit wouldn't kill her, and that was true in one sense. It wasn't toxic. But he lied when he said, 'Ye shall not surely die.' She surely did, and he knew he was deceiving her, beguiling her in her innocence," Rebekah observed.

"Yes, and he will do so again, only this time Satan will deceive those who are ready to be deceived. Suddenly those with rebellious hearts will seem to have a cause, not necessarily a just cause, but one that appears right on the surface. Those who do not love God supremely will follow this cause into perdition along with their father, the devil," Lev commented ruefully.

"While this is only a fuzzy view of the future, it is certainly enough for those who love the Lord to take heed and not to try to take matters into their own hands. No matter how tempting it may be or how reasonable it may appear on the outside, we will need to wait for the Lord to make it plain instead of jumping into the fray," the mellow and seasoned Benjamin wisely concluded.

Deborah interrupted the serious discussion. "It is time to celebrate with some of the choicest fruit from the Obadiah orchard and special cake and goodies from my kitchen. You won't find better eating anywhere!"

"You don't have to give me a second invitation," said Rebekah with a cheerful smile. "I've always known mother to serve the best food around."

They all laughed heartily and soon the table was crowded with succulent fruit and the aroma of fresh tea. After Benjamin offered the prayer, they began to enjoy the finest food paradise had to offer. As they were eating Lev observed, "Father Benjamin, I think that in working with all the flora of this earth you have gained insights about God's ways more than most of us."

"Don't forget, Lev, I study the Word of the Lord as well. We cannot be wise above what is written. Working with plants, I observe that everything has its proper time, and you must patiently wait for it. God works slowly, or so it often appears to us, but how beautiful He makes everything!"

After dinner, they talked into the night trying to gain as much insight as they could from the wisdom of Rebekah's parents. The Obadiahs had been God's faithful servants for many years, though they were young and vibrant in appearance.

Deborah was eager to add her input. "The coming days will only reveal what people are made of. God has known all along those who love themselves more than others, and He knows those who are waiting for a cause to rally around to gain prominence. He could have destroyed them long ago, but He has chosen to let them be revealed by their works to demonstrate what kind of people they really are. No one will fail to see the righteousness of God's judgments in this way."

Benjamin closed the evening with his observation. "Those who stand approved of God and Christ will be so much in harmony with God's arrangements that they will scarcely be aware of any trials or testing."

Lev and Rebekah realized they had talked too long to go home that night and decided to stay overnight with the Obadiahs. It would give them added fellowship.

"A word spoken in due season, how good is it!"
(Proverbs 15:23).

Chapter Seven

"Shall not the Judge of all the earth do right (Genesis 18:25)?" Many were repeating this verse of scripture to prove that no one who lives uprightly would be lost. How could people that had shown a love for Christ and God throughout the reign of Christ be lost? There were a considerable number who shared this conviction. They felt it did not seem right that people would be lost for what they did not do. Many could understand sins of commission, but they did not understand sins of omission. Their argument was that one could not fail by default.

Hans Mittel became a passionate speaker for the view that no one would be lost for merely *not* doing something, and many found comfort in such assurance. Christ would not condemn anyone who was not secretly a sinner. He assured people that Christ was too loving to let good people die. He asserted, "How good do you have to be in order to be considered good?"

Lev tried to stay out of this discussion. All that Hans Mittel was doing was raising a lot of dust to confuse people. It sounded good to preach Christ's love. However, Christ was not on trial.

Hans Mittel was gaining popularity among certain people, and he wanted to have a community meeting with Lev for an open forum discussion. Lev was reluctant to do so because there was so little merit to Hans' point of view. He was playing on people's emotions, encouraging an unwarranted security.

After repeated attempts to discourage him, Lev finally agreed to a small community meeting to discuss the matter. Hans was emboldened by Lev's unwillingness to debate the subject. He felt he would bring considerable comfort to many who were beginning to conclude that their fears were needless.

On the appointed evening, a large crowd gathered at the chapel to hear the discussion. Everyone knew that Lev was a notable figure, as well as a faithful servant of the King. Hans was an amiable person, well spoken and confident of the correctness of his position. The goodness and benevolence of people were the primary points Hans would use to win the sympathy of the audience.

Hans began by complimenting his opponent with a pleasant voice. "I want to first thank Lev for taking time out of his busy schedule to accept our invitation to discuss views that have been lying dormant for many years and now need to be addressed publicly. We all realize that Christ is the Righteous Judge, and we accept that his judgment will be just and true unequivocally. Christ does not need anyone to point him in the right direction. Christ has brought extraordinary blessings to the world, and he is unwilling that any should perish except that justice will require it. His righteousness and justice stand high above anyone's ability to question.

"Having said that, I would like to address a particular issue. I fear that many people are carrying a load of guilt unnecessarily. They are concerned that they are doomed as 'goats.' I desire to relieve them of that burden and give them hope and comfort. 'Shall not the Judge of all the earth do right?' (Genesis 18:25) We used to hear those who preached that God was fiendishly stoking the fires of hell for the unsaved. Usually, if you did not belong to their church, you were a likely candidate for hell-fire. Most of the folks who thought they were saved are here in the regeneration together with their supposedly unsaved brethren.

A "Goat" Class

"Does it not appear that we are going through a similar experience now? Only this time we conjure up the image of a 'goat' when we think someone is living below his privileges. We all agree that there will be some 'goats' because the Scriptures say so. But I submit that Christ has invested a lot of love into the human race and is unwilling that any should perish. He has enabled most people to survive throughout his reign, and he is in no hurry to dispatch many of them as 'goats.'

"Most people are kind and thoughtful and have been a joy to live with. They are hospitable, sensitive, and caring human beings. We cannot conceive of them as 'goats.' I am sure there must be some 'goats' out there, but I have not found any in my contacts. Why should people be faced with these unnecessary fears and worries? That seems to be a needless concern to all those who are at home in our loving, righteous society." Hans sat down amidst applause.

Lev slowly approached the podium and stood silently for a moment until the room quieted. "That speech certainly warmed our hearts, didn't it? By the way, I have a little surprise for you this evening. I have arranged for a very caring and loving person to be with us. It is my pleasure to introduce to you our Mother Eve. I thought she could answer Hans Mittel better than I, because she was formerly a perfect human being. Let us give her our careful attention." Eve had been sitting unnoticed in the audience. As she rose, she received a thunderous applause. Eve's eyes sparkled as she smiled at all her beloved children.

"Hans gave a very warm presentation, and I commend him for it. It lacked one thing, however, and that is it failed to address the principles that God has established as the habitation of His throne. Moses, the great Lawgiver, summed up the Law and

Jesus quotes him. 'Thou shalt love the Lord thy God with all thy heart, and with all thy soul, and with all thy mind. This is the first and greatest commandment. And the second is like unto it, Thou shalt love thy neighbor as thyself' (Matthew 22:37-39).

"In Eden, I failed this commandment. I wanted the forbidden fruit, because I thought it would give me something that God was withholding. I did not love my Creator enough to trust His wisdom and love for me. Because I sinned grievously, we all paid for it with suffering and dying. You see, I did not cease to be a good person. Adam and I lived very pure lives. We loved our children and made sacrifices for them. There was never an unkind word spoken between us. Your dear first father never once blamed me for the hardships we suffered after being driven out of Eden into the unfinished earth. In Eden we had everything. Then we had nothing. Yet, it was our punishment for disobeying."

A small, sad frown flitted briefly across her earnest face. "Once we were perfect. After we sinned we were still so nearly perfect you would not be able to find fault with us. But we were still under the curse and we died. You *cannot* live eternally unless you demonstrate that you 'love the Lord thy God with all thy heart, with all thy soul and all thy mind.' No matter how well we conduct our lives, being good is not enough. That is why those who do not show sufficient love for God will be deficient in their character. I made the first mistake, but I am determined not to make it again.

"As the days pass and the Millennial Age draws to an end, I entreat all of my children to consider their hearts. Search your heart for any lack of love and any unwillingness to give of yourself to the Lord or to your brothers and sisters."

There was a standing ovation when she finished. Lev stood up to say, "Mother Eve has said it all. I have nothing more to add."

Hans stood, his face solemn. With a humbled bow of his head, he slowly spoke, punctuating each word for emphasis. "Mother

Eve is right. Making an emotional case did not prove me right. My thanks to you, Mother Eve, for speaking to us straight from your heart."

Substandard Love Will Not Pass

Eve gave Hans a hug in front of everyone.

"The fact that Christ has kept the 'goats' alive through most of his reign is proof that he could keep them alive for an indefinite period. However, he will not do so. Christ has regenerated the whole human race, and again we have been on trial to see who will pass the test of perfect love. The test is really quite simple. We can show our love for Christ by showing love for our fellow men. May Christ bless each one of you. Thank you." With a face that seemed to embrace everyone, Eve concluded her remarks and took her seat.

Again, there was a standing ovation. Somehow the atmosphere was purified. Their discussion was filmed and would be played over and over until most people had seen it and understood the matter clearly. Mother Eve was the perfect person to speak on this subject.

Hans Mittel came to Eve after the discussion and thanked her again for clarifying the subject for him. He admitted to being heavily influenced by human philosophy and careless in his understanding of scripture.

"I guess it was human reasoning that got us into trouble in the first place. Well does the Bible say, 'There is a way which seemeth right unto a man, but the end thereof [are] the ways of death' (Proverbs 14:12). I was so convinced that I was right, and Lev knew I was wrong all along. I am glad I was stopped before I convinced others. I thank both of you for being so kind to this misguided fool."

Mother Eve kindly touched his face with her gentle hand. "My son, learn to trust not your own understanding. I did it once and see all the trouble it caused? I could not, in my wildest dreams, have imagined the pain and heartache that resulted because Satan beguiled me into thinking it would be all right. I had plenty of time to talk to the Lord about it, but I didn't. The knowledge I received was a bitter surprise. I immediately felt shame, guilt, fear, poverty, and the sentence of death. On a foolish impulse I made a fatal decision, the most painful and costly mistake ever made."

The audience stayed around to listen to Mother Eve. She was the most gracious lady, extravagantly beautiful outwardly, but more so inwardly. She spoke lovingly and with true wisdom to as many as she could. Finally Eve said, "It is late and we must go. My children, my life experiences are a tragedy made beautiful by Christ. Everything shall be restored. We are back in Eden eating from the trees of life and living even more graciously than before. My children have been restored, and the whole world is beautiful again. One thing remains. We must come into oneness with God. Jesus has mercifully kept us out of the hands of Divine Justice by serving as our Mediator, and he has prevented us from falling into the hands of the living God before we can measure up to His divine standards. Soon we will be called to stand in our own righteousness. Christ will no longer mediate between the living God and us. My dear ones, do not let anyone beguile you. It is a fearful thing to fall into God's hands if even a trace of sin remains in our hearts. I know from experience how God must immediately cast us off. His justice must be met, even though His love and mercy have provided every opportunity possible for us to succeed."

Failing in One Point

There followed a long silence. It was a moment where the past and present met. Tears flowed and a bond of love and tenderness grew. When Lev and Rebekah escorted Eve's departure, it was difficult to end the meeting. At last they entered their aircraft while the crowds stood waving tearfully—and foremost among them stood Hans Mittel.

This assembly did much to quiet the philosophy that God would not destroy good people who did not measure up to standards of perfect love. Eve made them realize that she was not a terribly wicked person at her sentencing, but a most noble and kind woman. She had failed only in one point, yet was still guilty. It was as James had written, "For whosoever shall keep the whole law, and yet offend in one point, he is guilty of all" (James 2:10).

They landed at Rebekah's house for the night. It was her great privilege to entertain Mother Eve. Though it was late and they were tired from the activities of the day, Eve thought she would enjoy some tea before retiring, and Lev joined them before going home. Rebekah had made some of her famous cake for Eve. Somehow their chat turned to Eve's first years after being driven out of Eden.

Eve closed her eyes for a moment. "You can't imagine how difficult it was. We built a little lean-to of sticks around a large tree. We collected grass for our bedding and then foraged for food. We did not know what was good for human consumption, but we learned quickly enough what was nourishing and what wasn't. We did not eat meat of any kind. Oh, how much we missed the trees of Eden!" A tear trickled down her cheek. "Adam learned to till the soil and plant seeds of plants that we found nourishing and tasty. That is how Cain became a farmer. We found that the milk of sheep was good for food, and we learned to make cheese. We found that sheep's wool was perfect for warmth and soon learned to weave cloth. Later on, Adam built a house of logs. Since it did not rain back then, the house did not have to be watertight.

"Animals did not become carnivores until after the Flood, so they were still docile and harmless. It was good that we did not have to be protected from them. They lived on the protein grass that we have restored to earth. Protein grass disappeared after the Flood, at least in sufficient quantities for the animals. Now that animals have it in plentiful measure, they have ceased being carnivores. Abel loved animals, and he tended our flock. Cain was very strong and preferred raising vegetables. Adam spent time developing metals for our use and was able to make copper. It was not until Tubalcain that iron was developed (Genesis 4:22).

"People were extremely intelligent in those days. We were still very near perfection. It is amazing how quickly we mastered the sciences. We were able to make pottery, certain metals, and instruments of music, weave clothing, and the list could go on. It took nearly fifty years before we were relatively comfortable again. We had to work for food from dawn until dark because of the curse placed upon us. Still, we were happy. God allowed us to live full and rich lives. It was not like in Eden, where every day was filled with pleasure and beauty. Most of all, we missed our daily communion with God and feeling His love and favor. Sin robbed us of so much.

"Our children never knew the close communion that we once enjoyed with God. They tried making atonement for sin, hoping this would return God's favor to them. Abel loved the Lord so much that he offered a precious lamb in sacrifice. Now we know why this pleased God, because it pictured how God was going to offer His own son, the Lamb of God, in sacrifice.

"Tragedy struck again when Cain, who worked harder than Abel, was not able to please God with his offerings of produce. We felt the sting of death in a bitter way. It is strange that acts of violence have followed religious men ever since then. Cain did not intend to murder his brother, but the blow or the fall after the blow caused cerebral bleeding and Abel died. We were all devastated. We were beginning to see what sin was really like. Of course, that was only a sampling of the rivers of blood that were yet to flow because of sin."

Lev and Rebekah sat enthralled as Eve recalled the past and made it come alive to them. Eve had such a gifted manner of speaking that she held their attention completely. It was getting late and they feared they were imposing upon her.

Rebekah said, "I am afraid we will have you all worn out with trying to learn of the past. I could listen to you all night, Mother Eve. Forgive us for being so inconsiderate."

Wanting an Assurance of God's Favor

"It is always a joy for me to recall the past. In my former life, all my children used to sit at my feet while I told them stories of the past," Eve said. "But they always wanted some assurance of a return of God's favor. All I could tell them was that God had promised 'the seed of the woman' would some day bruise the serpent's head (Genesis 3:15). Little did I know of God's wonderful plan of redemption."

"Did Adam ever blame you for eating the forbidden fruit?" asked Lev.

"No, Adam was noble beyond words. He suffered silently. Yet, we did have a full and rewarding life together. It is wonderful to be the mother and father of the whole human race. We had the love and respect of everyone. We did not yet have the Law that was given to Israel, but it was written in our hearts. All were raised with these values and the community of people knew no war in those days. It was not until we died that fallen angels began to materialize and fill the earth with violence (Genesis 6:2, 5). That is when evil spread over the earth. God preserved a line of pure Adamic stock through it all, however, and the fallen angels were prevented from marrying into people of this lineage. That is why Noah was perfect in his generation (Genesis 6:9). He was pure in his lineage to Adam. The angels were never authorized to marry the daughters of men. Consequently, all the progeny of the angels were destroyed in the Flood."

"I could listen to you all night, Mother Eve, but I am afraid we are taking advantage of you while we get the story of the first world before the Flood," Rebekah interjected.

"Why don't you spend a couple days with me in Eden?" Eve invited. "Adam would be pleased to be with you, I am certain. As you know firsthand from building our homes, we have the very finest accommodations. There is no place more beautiful than the Garden of Eden!"

"Lev, how can we say 'no' to such an offer?" Rebekah said enthusiastically.

Lev replied, "We have nothing to hinder our acceptance, so we would be delighted to come for a visit."

"Wonderful, Lev! I know Adam will enjoy your company. We often speak of you both and the day we met on our first day of life from the sleep of death."

Lev finished the last cup of tea with another piece of cake and said, "I will leave the aircraft parked on your pad. I need to walk home and review all the wonderful events of the day. Mother Eve, having you address Hans Mittel was absolutely what everyone needed to be convinced. You were perfect. God blessed this day."

"My children, it is the end of a perfect day. I thank you for making it all possible. I will see you in the morning. Shalom!"

After saying goodnight to Mother Eve and Rebekah, Lev walked home under a full moon. His mind was still savoring the day's events as he lifted his heart in prayer.

The next morning Lev arose eager to take in the blessings of a new day. He packed his things for a two-day visit in Eden and quickly walked to Rebekah's home. He found the women bright and cheerfully talking. Breakfast was ready and the smell of tea permeated the air. They enjoyed breakfast before leaving for the chapel from where they planned to leave for Eden. Eve was eager to visit the chapel.

Mother Eve's presence at the chapel delighted everyone, and they gave her an outpouring of love and affection. When asked if she would participate in the services, she said, "Nothing gives me greater pleasure than hearing my children praise the Lord. I would prefer to join you in your worship. Thank you."

After the services ended, everyone flocked around their First Mother to greet her personally. A few who were at the meeting the previous evening wanted to express their gratitude for her wise contributions. It was difficult to break away with the adoring crowds pressing in upon her. At last they were able to lift off for Eden.

"Eastward in Eden"
(Genesis 2:8).

Chapter Eight

Adam was waiting to receive Eve, Lev and Rebekah with outstretched arms.

"Welcome to Eden, my friends! I hear your meeting went very well! Your journey proved a victory for the truth."

Adam was the image of physical perfection and beauty. No one had to be told that he was God's creation and Christ had recreated him. His presence commanded immediate respect. Adam invited them to come in and be refreshed from their journey with the same eagerness that Abraham had manifested when welcoming the three angels to share his hospitality (Genesis 18:2).

"We often speak of you both when we reminisce of our first day of life in our new Paradise in Eden. We will always be thankful to you and your family for building our magnificent garden homes. You and your family will always be welcome guests in Eden."

"Definitely!" Eve concurred. "Come! Let us sit down at the table. Adam has prepared a feast of refreshments for us!" Eve exclaimed.

After Adam offered a prayer of thanks, he passed the fruit of Paradise, and it seemed especially good to the weary travelers. Once the dishes had been passed around, the conversation turned serious, reviewing their meeting with Hans Mittel in the chapel at Beersheva.

"Eve and I have been living in determined resolve since our return to life. We did not want a day to go by without having done something to honor our Lord and to bless our children. I think Eve answered Hans Mittel very well, and most people understood her presentation clearly. You have both had a lot of experience along this line. What is a good way to explain why love must labor and faith must work?"

Rebekah spoke up first. "Love and faith both are powerful forces, with love being the most powerful force in the universe. Yet love is only expressed by what it does. God not only gave us life. He gave us an abundant life—with food, beauty, health, dominion, music, and countless other blessings. God's love was manifested in what He did for us after He created us. He doesn't need faith, because He has all knowledge and everything is under His control. However, knowing that God did so many things for us, we must have faith that He will do everything He has promised."

"God is Love"

Lev continued, "God is love. There is no meanness in His nature. We are told, 'Have I any pleasure at all that the wicked should die? saith the Lord GOD: and not that he should return from his ways, and live?' (Ezekiel 18:23). Justice comes into play here. God's justice is also perfect and all who don't meet the requirements of perfect love for God or their fellow men must be cut off from life. If God allowed those who did not have a laboring love and a working faith to live, He would be permitting weakness in His Kingdom."

"Yes, of course," said Eve. "That is why God tested our love for Him. He could have interceded and prevented me from eating the forbidden fruit. He could have exposed the serpent as a liar immediately as soon as he tried to deceive me. But then I would expect God to intercede every time I was exposed to temptation. I hope I will not believe another lie again. Once is enough! God wants strong and disciplined followers who have faith in Him. I did not demonstrate faith in my Maker."

Adam said, "Many seem to feel that God might lower the standard to let those who want life to live even though they don't completely measure up to His perfect law."

"How could He?" replied Rebekah. "He cannot have a double standard. If perfect love is required of one, it must be required of all. He cannot show partiality. We know that when the angels sinned, they were cast out of heaven. Everyone in heaven had to demonstrate that they loved righteousness and hated iniquity. So it must be on earth. People were given abundant opportunities throughout the Millennial Age to show their love for God and Christ in countless ways. If they were not doing something for others or for the general good and overlooked these opportunities, they showed insensitivity to others and toward God's plan of reconciliation. You know no one was sick or too tired to get involved. They all had perfect health. No one was too poor to help. Everyone was rich and secure. Everyone has had plenty of opportunities. No one can say, 'I didn't have the time.'"

"Right," added Lev. "The workweek of the average person has never required more than twenty percent of their time. That left more than ample time to do things for others. There was no law against doing more than twenty percent. We all had the strength and vitality necessary. No sacrifices were called for that were too difficult. The only reason they were left undone is because people *chose* to leave them for others to carry out."

Adam listened intently to the comments with satisfaction. He said, "I've observed how selfishness works in the human heart of man about as long as anyone. Starting with my son Cain, when God inquired about Abel whom he had slain, he said, 'Am I my brother's keeper?' That was Cain's way of disowning his responsibility to his brother. He didn't confess to God who knows all things, 'I killed my brother. I am sorry. I didn't mean my actions to result in his death.' From then until now the human heart has been deceitful if not honestly guarded, and the one it deceives first is oneself. God is not fooled for one minute by all these ploys."

Separating Work to Be Done

Rebekah sipped her tea thoughtfully. "When Christ is done screening those who truly love God, it will be a most wonderful service when he separates the two classes. The 'goats' would not be truly happy in the same world with the 'sheep.'"

"I don't want to make the same mistake twice," Eve sighed.

Adam said, "We both plunged the world into sin, death, suffering and sorrow. But this time it will be different. Everyone will die for his own failing."

Eve said, "Let's not dwell on the negative. Now that we're refreshed, let's walk in Eden. It is very much like it was at first, though the fountain of water coming from the earth is much smaller. It is so crystal clear that you can see fish and other life in it distinctly. It is such a joy to be home again, eating from the trees of life. You have no idea what a blessing it is for me to be partaking of them. When I awakened and realized that I was back in Eden, my heart jumped for joy. Then to find Adam alive and so young again with all our children, I knew our sins were forgiven. Christ made it all happen."

A little lion cub came up to them as they strolled through the serene setting. The mother looked on unconcerned while the cub frolicked about them. Adam stooped to scratch his tummy and then they passed on.

Rebekah asked, "Do you have any serpents here?"

"Oh no!" Eve replied.

"Did you have mosquitoes in Eden?" asked Rebekah.

"No, of course not," said Eve. "We were never bitten there. It was not until we were driven out of Eden that our trouble with bugs started. We had no mosquitoes then either. We suspect they came after the Flood. Occasionally an ant would crawl on us and bite us—nothing very serious, just a welt."

"Where did mosquitoes come from?" asked Lev.

"We think that after the Flood the devil and the fallen angels started experimenting with different life forms. They could not materialize anymore so they tried genetic experiments, and that may be how some of these pesky bugs came about," said Adam.

"So all they did was to add to human misery," observed Lev.

"That's about it," observed Adam. "And when the fallen angels were confined to earth, they only seemed obsessed with getting control of mankind. Before the Flood they could materialize and dominate men. After the Flood they used false religions or ideologies to control people."

Rebekah wondered aloud, "Maybe that's why all these things the demons brought upon men were eliminated when Christ set up his Kingdom in power and great glory."

"Did you ever travel out of Eden before you were driven out?" asked Lev.

"Eden was uniquely placed," said Adam. "From the central geyser the water formed into four rivers and flowed out of Eden. The waters fell over cliffs and through mountain passes. Actually, there was only one way leading out of Eden by land. You could use a boat to get in and out using the rivers, but we never even thought of that. When we were driven out of Eden, we realized we would have to do a lot of work on the unfinished earth—but, guess what! When I awakened, that work was all done. And someone," he winked at Lev and Rebekah, "made some great improvements building houses that don't even look like houses, but are still comfortable day and night. It is just beautiful, Lev."

Given the Gift of Life

"You both gave the human race life! It is the least we could do in return," said Rebekah. "When my father heard he was to plant the Eden Paradise, he was the happiest man. My mother, also. They didn't leave a stone unturned trying to make it like the original Eden. They consulted with Cain and Abel and your oldest children to see what they remembered from your descriptions of Eden, because their memory was nearly perfect."

Eve said, "Of course they couldn't duplicate everything that the Creator had planted there. The trees of life were provided by divine grace, and we have them from seeds that the angels preserved for us. They are the joy of the whole world now. You must have perfect food for perfect people. As soon as we lost access to the trees of life, we felt the effects of death working on us."

"We did not have the common diseases. That came much later," Adam added. "Remember, I lived 930 years! (Genesis 5:5.) We simply grew older gradually with wrinkling skin, weaker with more aches and pains, and slower in our movements. None of the horrible diseases that afflicted our children were known before the Flood. But the curse God put upon us was real. We saw evidences of change and decay in our bodies very quickly. We could only dream of eating from the trees of life again. Yet, God was merciful and gracious and gave us a busy and satisfying life together. We were able to begin one part of our commission—'to fill the earth.' It did not rain before the Flood, and mist from the earth watered the ground (Genesis 2:4-6). We lived by the river, because the best crops grew along the riverbank. Of course, there were many springs that fed into smaller streams also, and all the water was pure, except in the oceans. We did not harm the earth until the nations began to industrialize the world."

"You are absolutely right! You should have seen the clouds of smog we created with industrial pollution. We farmed with chemicals, killed weeds with chemicals, and raised animals in pitiful conditions. We poisoned the earth trying to produce food. Then we added radioactive atomic energy and atomic weapons to our folly. It was 'penny wise and pound foolish' in farming, and total irresponsibility in creating energy and weapons of destruction," said Lev.

"I understand that if the Lord had not stopped the carnage in the earth, there would have been 'no flesh saved' (Matthew 24:22)," responded Adam. "Thankfully, the Lord intervened before the madness of men achieved human annihilation. Ignorance, religious bigotry, superstition, and an endless capacity to hate almost destroyed the human race. I could not conceive how degraded men could become. I still look back in history and find it hard to believe that my children became so depraved."

"Me too," Eve added. "It left me trembling when I learned the truth confirmed by people that experienced such barbarism. How the human heart must have shriveled!"

"Only the Lord has been able to take this tangled mass of humanity, put his Spirit within them, turn them inside out, and put love and righteousness in their hearts. I have seen it happen before my eyes, and I never cease to marvel at it," said Rebekah.

An Assyrian Guest

The third river, formerly called Hiddekel, was smaller now. As they walked along its banks, they saw a man who had paddled upstream. He had pulled his canoe out of the water and was resting against it. When the group walked up, they startled him. He exclaimed, "Shalom! I hope I haven't intruded. I was just following the river to its source. I must be near it now."

"Welcome, my friend, to Eden. The source of the river is here. I am Adam. This is my former wife, Eve, and our guests Rebekah and Lev Aron. The earth is the Lord's, and you are welcome in Eden."

"This is a big surprise for me! I am Omar, from Assyria," he said as he arose to greet this honorable company. "I heard that if I followed this river to its source I might come to Eden. But meeting Adam and Eve, the first parents of all humanity, is overwhelming. I feel unworthy of this privilege. Please, if I am intruding, I will leave."

"No, no, please stay," Eve reassuringly encouraged. "You must be tired."

"Yes indeed, Omar, you will be my guest tonight. Lev and Rebekah are staying, and we enjoy company. They designed the new Eden with accommodations for many guests, so you may sleep in Paradise tonight," said Adam.

"Why, thank you. I am honored and most unworthy," Omar replied.

"You may leave your canoe where it is, but bring your overnight things with you. It is late in the day, so come with us and refresh yourself," said Adam.

All the birds were finding their roosts for the night. Omar was overwhelmed at the beauty of Eden and the homes of Adam and Eve.

Adam served hot tea and fruit from Paradise, and they settled into the evening's pleasures. They sat in the comfort of the garden home, its rooms gently washed by indirect illumination. Omar was overcome with gratitude to be a guest of the first human pair.

When asked about his background, Omar said, "I lived during the time of Sennacherib and was a warrior in his army. We were busy terrorizing and pillaging the nations. We were notoriously cruel and arrogant. When nations resisted us, we conquered them and abused them without mercy. I witnessed the death of hundreds of men skinned alive. I can never forget those scenes—they haunt me to this day. I have met these people in the resurrection, and they still quiver remembering their tortured end. It was absolutely inhuman. Fortunately, I was never engaged in the actual procedure, but I dared show no sympathy with the victims, although I hated what I saw.

An Army Destroyed in a Night

"The same thing happened to the Jews in Hezekiah's time," he continued. "They resisted Sennacherib's forces, so he was determined to make an example of them. You know the story how his whole army was destroyed in a night—one hundred and eighty-five thousand men (II Kings 19:35). Sennacherib escaped, but he had suffered irreparable loss. I had been sent as a scout to another area that night. When I returned to Jerusalem to give my report, I saw only the carcasses of our army. The Jews were busy stripping the dead, so they did not notice me. I rode away before I was apprehended."

Eve said, "So you were a witness to the barbarisms of that time."

"Yes, I was. I killed on the battlefield, and I kicked and punched our prisoners, and I'm thankful I was spared having to meet those victims in the regeneration. The Lord's ways are equal. Those who did such things seem to have scarred their consciences. Many of them were destroyed at the end of a hundred years. I guess there are limits to depravity."

Adam said, "How dreadful! We have spent sleepless nights hearing of the cruelty of our children to each other. We saw the effects of sin in our time, but never did we imagine the cruelty and barbarism that would take place on the earth." Tears were running down his cheeks as he spoke.

Eve started to speak, but she couldn't hold back the tears and excused herself to gather her composure.

"I am sorry to have brought such sadness to you. It has been a heavy weight on my heart," Omar said. "You never forget such things. It is one thing to hear about this, but quite another to witness those scenes in all their ugliness. I have had many nightmares over these memories. But these things must never be forgotten."

"We bear full responsibility for sin in the earth," said Adam. "We would never have disobeyed if we could have foreseen the effects of our actions. Now, of course, all history is open to us, and we see what sin can do when it is released."

Lev said, "Sin is like a small snowball rolling downhill. It picks up speed, size, and momentum as it descends. There is a lesson here for all of us. We cannot have any sympathy for sin in ourselves. If, at the end of the thousand years, we witness the death of some, it will be because they were not loving God supremely."

Omar was startled at Lev's statement. He said, "You really mean that, don't you? You are saying the greatest failure will be in failing to love God supremely, and I suppose the second will be in failing to love our neighbor as ourselves."

"Exactly, Omar. None will gain everlasting life who fails in love," said Lev.

"I never saw it that way before!" Omar exclaimed. "Now that you state it so clearly, I can understand that failure to love God supremely is the way of death. I should have known that long ago. I guess I needed this information, and that is why I was led to you. You know that I come from a pagan nation and knew little about the Lord in my former life. I learned something of the power of the living God when I saw our army annihilated. I began to have some fear of Him thereafter. Although the Lord spared his life, Sennacherib never again ventured near Israel in his exploits. I asked him what happened that night, and he wouldn't even discuss about it. His end came just as Isaiah said it would. His two sons killed him while he was worshipping the false god Nisroch (2 Kings 19:37)."

False Gods Are Gone

Adam said, "You apparently are familiar with the Scriptures now. Aren't you glad to know all these false gods are gone forever? Cruel demons created these terrible deities to gain control of people through religion. The evil spirits are all destroyed, thank God. Only Satan remains to be loosed."

"Why didn't He destroy Satan along with the demons?" asked Omar.

"Because God is going to let Satan out of his prison to deceive those who will follow him," answered Lev. "God is not going to have anyone in His everlasting Kingdom who will be deceived by Satan. He reserved Satan to test the loyalty of His subjects. Those weak enough to be misled are not going to pass the test."

"Oh my," intoned Omar. "I am afraid many of my friends have a more relaxed idea of salvation. They think that Christ loves them too much to let them fall short of salvation. They feel if they were good enough to live through the Millennium, they are good enough to live forever."

Eve said, "That is what happens when you let false ideas replace truth. This was the stock and trade of all false religions. Ministers used to show great largess in opening the gates of heaven to their parishioners. But God never let anyone into heaven except those who followed the Lamb very closely. Nevertheless, the churches succeeded in fostering false hopes in people's hearts."

"Yes, our former god Nisroch promised heaven to all our warriors. Yet we all died and slept until Jesus awakened us," Omar confided. "Tell the people what they want to hear—they won't know they've been misled until it is too late."

Lev commented, "We are all older and we should be wiser now, especially when we know Satan will be released out of his prison. We should be slow to do anything unless we know God or Christ approves it."

"Amen, to that. No more quick judgments for me," Eve said.

Everyone laughed at her comment, although it underscored a truth.

It was getting late, so Eve and Rebekah decided to retire for the night. Omar was tired, too. He had paddled his canoe a long distance that day, so Adam showed him to his room. "You should sleep soundly, my son. If you need anything, let me know. I will be up at six o'clock, but you may sleep as long as you like. Breakfast will be ready whenever you get up. Shalom."

Lev was also tired, but before going to bed, he wanted to know when the chapel services would begin. They had built a chapel in Eden large enough for visitors. It was well attended because Adam was the chaplain most of the time.

Adam Is the Chaplain

Omar and Lev were awake early to greet Adam who was preparing for the service that morning. They drank fresh hot tea and fruit juice to start the day. Two kids of goats were frolicking outside their home, while the birds provided an assortment of songs. It was what one might expect in Paradise.

Adam decided to give the kids fruit from the trees of life for a little treat. They ate it voraciously. He said, "It doesn't work for them as it does for us. They still get old and die. If they lived forever, we wouldn't have little kids coming into the world. So life must come and life must go in the lower animal world, much like the plants. They are all part of the natural processes of the earth. We as humans are blessed to have the promise of eternity."

"Do you wish to come to the chapel with us this morning, Omar?" asked Adam.

"Yes, of course!" he replied enthusiastically. "I hear you are the chaplain, and who could serve better than our first father?"

"Great! As soon as the ladies join us, we will walk through Eden to the chapel," said Adam.

Soon Eve appeared with Rebekah looking refreshed and eager for the blessings of the day. "We aren't late, are we?" asked Eve.

"No, indeed—we have time for a nice walk. Take an extra piece of fruit with you. We may find some hungry animals along the way," said Adam.

Sure enough, no sooner had they started out than a raccoon was waiting for them like a little masked bandit. Omar gave him some fruit. The raccoon examined it carefully and then started eating.

"He is here almost every morning, the little beggar," exclaimed Adam.

Today was a special day, for standing not far from their path was a mother elephant and her seldom-seen baby.

"Who has something for guests?" asked Adam.

"I'll feed the baby," said Rebekah. "Lev, you feed the mother."

The little elephant came eagerly for the delicious fruit while the mother paused, but then accepted the offering Lev held with his outstretched arm. They both happily seized the fruit with their trunks and thrust it into their mouths. Adam waited until the last. As he approached the chapel, he spotted a llama eating grass. It also eagerly came for some of the fruit.

As they entered the chapel, a crowd was already gathered waiting for their first parents to welcome them to Eden. A small orchestra was already playing hymns of praise.

Adam and Eve made an effort to introduce their guests, but it was clear they were the ones everyone wanted to see and greet. It was wonderful being unnoticed and insignificant, overshadowed by the first man and woman of God's creation. Omar was so inspired by it all, he started humming the music in his strong baritone.

No one thought about daily business. With one voice, they praised God from whom all blessings flow. Adam called on Lev for the opening prayer and then asked Omar, Eve, Rebekah and Lev to sing as a quartet an old well-known hymn, "How Great Thou Art!" The whole congregation joined in the chorus, and the room vibrated with joy. After a lovely service that held everyone in rapt attention, Adam closed in prayer. This was not a prayer read out of a book as was done in yesteryear, but a living prayer.

The crowd lingered and was welcomed to stroll through Eden. There were plenty of trees of life throughout the garden, and they could eat as much as they wished.

Eve invited their guests back to her house where she served breakfast. Omar felt he was in heaven. In his fondest dreams he had not anticipated such royal treatment. Tears streamed down his cheeks when he left for his canoe. He had been influenced and encouraged by the love shown him, a perfect stranger, but as Eve said, "You know we are all family." She gave him a gentle farewell kiss on the cheek.

"Great is the LORD, and greatly to be praised
in the city of our God, in the mountain of his holiness.
Beautiful for situation, the joy of the whole earth,
is mount Zion, on the sides of the north,
the city of the great King.
God is known in her palaces for a refuge"
(Psalm 48:1-3).

Chapter Nine

Lev was back home in Israel for many months. Everything appeared to have quieted down in the earth. No one seemed to be talking about the separation of the 'sheep' and 'goats' because it had been covered in considerable depth. Most people thought the die was already cast. They did not think it was likely that the 'goats' would decide to become 'sheep,' or vice versa.

Lev became concerned that things were too calm outwardly. He was sure the Millennium was ending, but everything seemed too tranquil. The philosophy that Christ had too much love to send anyone into second death who was good and law-abiding was not even being mentioned anymore. It made him wonder— could it be that everyone was accepting and acquiescent to arrangements as they were?

He had also heard nothing from the Ancients. Lev knew that when Christ turned the kingdom over to the Father it might end the services of the Ancients, although this had not been revealed. It would certainly be a time of transition. Patience would be required until the world would operate smoothly without the rule of Christ, the Mediator, and the Ancients. People would be directly responsible to the Father and would have to be extra careful. Absolute holiness would be required of everyone all the time.

Early in the evening while he was settling down into his studies, Lev received a call from a woman, Esther Blank. "Shalom, Lev—you don't know me, but I wonder if you could spare a moment of your time to consider an idea some of us have. Mind you, this is only a humble thought, but I think it might be worth consideration."

"How can I refuse a humble thought?" Lev responded with a friendly chuckle.

"We all know we are at the end of the Millennium," Esther began. "The rule of Christ as Mediator will soon end, and the government of earth will come back into human hands at some point. Jerusalem has been its capital and has served us well. Why not move the capital to a new place and make it more accessible to the whole world? Jerusalem is such an old city. Most buildings are old and outdated, and it isn't laid out with wide streets. It is beautiful in its own way, but lacks the dynamics of an architecturally updated city. Additionally, Jerusalem has endured more bloodshed in its history than almost any other city. Why continue to have it as the headquarters of the world?"

Lev was taken by surprise. "What you say may be true, Esther, but we have had the longest period of peace since Jerusalem has become the capital of the world. And isn't that what 'Salem' means, 'City of Peace'?"

"Yes, of course!" she retorted. "But how can you erase its bloody history? For centuries Jerusalem has known war. The last war was Armageddon in which millions of lives perished. We will always be reminded of the horror there."

"Esther, I died in Armageddon defending Jerusalem against impossible odds, but I look on it as a great victory for righteousness and truth. Why would I want to forget the battle that ushered in righteousness?"

"They were burying the dead for months. It was so grotesque. Such massive carnage is not a pleasant memory."

The Forces of Hatred Were Defeated

"It depends on how you look at it, Esther," said Lev. "The forces of hate and unrighteousness were defeated there. That was the most savage and unjust war ever waged. The nations swept in against Israel to take Jerusalem away from the people of Israel. God had given them the land of Israel as their rightful heritage, and the nations were determined to take it away."

"Yes, Lev, but still the fact remains that much blood was spilled there. Shouldn't we have a more peaceful city to look up to?"

"The fact that blood was spilled there and other places must always be remembered. We never want to forget the permission of evil. It will be as an odious smoke on our horizon to be remembered forever."

"Yes, so it will," Esther agreed. "But I have a vision of a world capital built where no city has existed before, on land not washed with blood. That would be a true symbol of peace."

"If there is such a place, it would not demonstrate that peace was not attained without sacrifice. Christ had to pay the price for sin and then had to engage his limitless power to remove it. Peace did not just happen."

Esther responded firmly. "We would never wish to take away from the great cost that sin made necessary, and I fully concur that Christ made it all possible. We will always remember Golgotha for the cross, and all Christ's faithful followers throughout the past who were lights in a world of darkness."

"I guess I sound negative to your idea because I am, Esther," Lev finally responded. "I am sure your idea is well intentioned, but it certainly is not an idea made in heaven. Were you asked to find a new capital for the world?"

Esther hesitated, "Well, no."

"Then why are you volunteering to change the seat of world government?"

"Because we are entering a new age when mankind will begin some form of self-rule. Why not start with a fresh slate—a place not washed in blood?"

Lev spoke more firmly. "Christ is now Ruler of heaven and earth. He will no longer serve as our Mediator between God and man, but he will still have all power in heaven and earth. Earth will be left with some self-government, but mostly it will be the rule of law and everyone will be responsible for keeping that law perfectly."

"Surely we have had the rule of law throughout Christ's reign. How will it be any different then?" Esther asked.

"The law has been enforced by spiritual forces. I know that personally. When I returned to life I ran into an old enemy of mine and tried to injure him with a well-aimed blow. My arm was paralyzed immediately, and I saw it work many times with others the same way to prevent violence. That was the law being enforced—no one could hurt or destroy in all Christ's Kingdom. We soon learned not to break the law. Today no one would use violence. We know from experience that it is not permitted. At the same time we know that the spiritual police force is still in place. That is what secures our world."

"Do you mean that shortly, when Christ's reign as Mediator is complete, the spiritual force will be removed?"

"Yes, and on top of that Satan will be loosed out of his prison to deceive any who will follow him."

"You mean anyone will be free to be tempted by Satan's sweet deceptions?" queried Esther further.

"Why else would Satan be freed from his prison?"

"Getting back to the purpose of my call, Lev, you know that the Lord did not allow David to build His temple because David was a man of bloodshed and war, don't you?"

Mt. Zion Seat of Authority

"Yes, Esther, I am aware of that. Yet, the Lord gave Jerusalem into David's hands, and it is still called the City of David. Not only so, but David built his ruling house on Mt. Zion. God promised him a son who would rule on Zion's Hill forever. Additionally, He allowed the Jewish Temple to be built on Mt. Moriah. It was a place where the blood of bulls and goats were offered to typify the better sacrifices instituted by Christ. Remember, blood was spilled there with God's knowledge. It is a reminder for us that without the shedding of blood on God's altar, there is no remission of sin (Hebrews 9:22)."

"I am afraid I called the wrong person. Everyone else was very receptive to the idea."

"That is the trouble with going by polls. There is no basis in scripture for your idea of building a new and glorious capital city. Jerusalem is our capital. Why change it?"

"You didn't listen to a word I said, Lev. Anyway, it is only a humble suggestion. There is no plan to stage a revolt to have it our way," Esther confessed.

"I'm glad to hear that!"

"Thank you for your time, Lev. I still cherish the idea. It seems so right."

"Shalom! Wait upon the Lord, Esther."

Lev hung up the phone hoping that would be the end of the matter. Maybe this was just a random idea and it would die by itself. Lev returned to his studies and soon dismissed the whole matter as a non-event. He had a new project to work on for tomorrow's meeting with his brother Jake and Jake's team. Lev was thinking about the new project late into the night when he finally realized what time it was.

When Lev arrived at work the next morning, he found several people including Jake had been contacted about building a new capital. He said, "I received a call yesterday suggesting the same thing."

Jake observed, "This must be quite a movement, and the devil has not yet been released. I am afraid I was short with my caller. I told her that when God or Christ asks that we build a new capital, call then and we would be glad to work on it."

Another person said, "I told my caller that I loved Jerusalem and would not betray the Beloved City. The suggestion leaves me cold."

Lev began to think that the idea was not a widespread one, but rather a little circle of people who were trying to get endorsement by someone prominent to the public. The negative responses should have quickly squelched the idea. To his immense satisfaction no more was heard of a new capital in later days. It was amazing how often people with ambitions, however well intended, were tempted to come up with ideas and causes they could initiate. Lev wondered if this indicated a love of self more than a love of God.

The project they were undertaking had been carefully planned. The arguments they used to face when imperfect planning was the rule ceased when perfect minds challenged them.

According to Lev's figures, the Millennium was within weeks from ending now. He expected it to be in the fall of that year, but still he was surprised that everything was so peaceful. There were no raging debates. Everyone was very calm. Regardless, he knew that a certain judgment was looming up before them—the 'sheep' and the 'goats' were to be separated.

The Great Lawgiver Makes a Visit

Then early one evening Lev received a telephone call from Moses saying he would be flying in the next afternoon and wished to spend an evening with him. It was a great honor to have such a distinguished guest. Lev asked, "Shall I invite guests or do you want a private meeting?"

"I would prefer a private discussion with you, Lev. Shalom."

The Ancients frequently visited communities now, and people were using the opportunity to learn from them firsthand. Moses was the Great Lawgiver, and it was generally believed he would again write a perfect Law that God would give them after the thousand years were ended and the people entered into the bonds of the New Covenant. Only this time, there would be no provisions made for breaking the law as with the Old Law Covenant. That New Law was to have been written in their hearts during Christ's reign.

At the time appointed, Moses' silver aircraft settled down on Lev's pad. Lev hurried out to welcome him. "Shalom," Lev greeted.

Moses, who had once died at one hundred and twenty years old, was still in full vigor of manhood with keen vision. Now he was a perfect specimen of humanity, and his dignity and stature were very commanding. Lev almost felt like bowing in his presence, but he knew better.

"Shalom, Lev," Moses said. "You have a very pleasant home, and I am happy to spend the night. I am sorry this is not an occasion for inviting other guests, but I want some private time with you."

"Nothing could please me more, Moses. Come in and make yourself at home and I will get you some refreshments."

Lev prepared a bowl of fruit salad and green salad, as well as some fresh steamed vegetables that he knew Moses really liked. Rebekah had sent over a cake and some cookies for them.

"Lev, I did not come down for a fine meal, although I am grateful for it. I have come to see you because the end of the Millennium is at hand and some changes are coming in earth's affairs. The Lord is not going to remove us from office as soon as some would like and that may cause a stir. You have been in general contact with people more than we are in Jerusalem. What do you hear?"

"Recently a lady called me asking about creating a new world capital when the Ancients leave office. Jerusalem is a grand city, but she feels too much blood has been spilled there. They want to make a fresh start in government with a new, modern city that will dazzle the world."

"How interesting," Moses mused.

"Then at work I found out that several others had called people at Jake's place of employment with much the same pitch. However, no one agreed with their thinking, and it seems to have quieted down."

The Love of Power and Visibility

"It may be that some people are looking for a cause with which to identify," answered Moses. "Once people have been prominent in the world, it is hard to get the love of power and visibility out of their blood. I was in the courts of Pharaoh until forty years old. After I defeated the Ethiopian army, I rose to prominence as the savior of the nation. I tried to lead my people to freedom. Yes, that was a good cause. Yet, the people of Israel viewed me as an Egyptian and my efforts were doomed to failure. I had to flee for my life. I wanted so much to deliver Israel from Egyptian bondage, but my intense desires actually disqualified me from that position. I went from the courts of Pharaoh to tending sheep on the backside of the desert for forty years. I was thoroughly humbled and could not in my fondest dreams imagine the Lord wanted me then, at eighty years of age, to lead Israel to the Promised Land. I even tried to get out of the responsibility, for I was feeling totally inadequate. But the Lord thought I was ready for the job, when I was sure I was not. I know how strong ambitions of all kinds are the cause of so much trouble, and people find these ambitions die hard, especially if they nurture them secretly in their hearts."

"I understand, Moses. Various groups and institutions secretly were filled with unholy ambitions in the past. Religious leaders wanted to rule the world from the church or mosque, because they felt they had religious goodness to bestow. When they could not accomplish this alone, they tried uniting with the state. Then the worst oppressions followed. Schools wanted to influence the world through the classroom. Politicians wanted to influence the world through politics. The rich sought power in the world through riches. The merchants tried to use merchandise to gain their place in the world. Yes, every field of endeavor made its bid for power. The last group to come forward to save the world was science. It was to succeed where others failed. Yet science unleashed the greatest terrors. Thankfully, God saved us when all the others were destroying us."

Moses reflected a moment and said, "Lev, when Satan is released shortly, people will have a lot of latent longings to which he will appeal. Those who haven't flushed these from within will be very vulnerable. But that is not our concern just yet. We still have a 'goat' class that is to be revealed shortly. I cannot tell you the exact time, but you are a good student and know it is very soon. I did not come to tell you the date, but we must continue to try to hold up the divine mirror that reveals the true image of the heart. Too many are singing of Jesus' love for them. They think this will replace the lack of love in their heart."

"You are so right, Moses. I've confronted this attitude throughout the age, but I am afraid it is the sweet song some want to believe. It is kind of late in the day to change the mindset of people."

"No one is more deceived than the one who deceives himself," Moses added. "However, people are at the point of physical perfection, and they are more awake to reality. Your recent exchange with Hans Mittel and Eve was very forceful in exposing the error in his thinking. What we want to do is to play this incident on international television as a last reminder that Christ will destroy those failing in love for God and their fellow men."

"You have my permission, if that is what you want. You didn't have to fly here for that. Everything we do and stand for is out in the open. The same would be true of Eve, I am sure. Hans Mittel may be embarrassed by it, but he would also agree with us now."

"We knew that, of course, Lev. We are grateful for your cooperation. We have grown to have great trust and confidence in you. No, the Ancients are looking beyond when the 'sheep' and 'goats' are separated. When Satan is loosed and we remain in office longer than some people would like us to be, we are not going to explain our actions to anyone. We want you to be our spokesperson. We will be operating at Christ's request, but we will not be free to state that fact. As our spokesperson, you may find it quite a challenge, because Satan will press for a change in government control. Of course, he will not be able to fault Christ, but Satan will manage to fault us for staying in power through others. You will face the rising demand for our leaving office. We will remain silent all the while. We have our instructions from Christ."

Facing Those Pushing for Change

"You know, Moses, I will serve anywhere and in any way our King desires. I do not mind facing those pushing for change. I have faced any number of people who have had a different opinion. As long as I know I am being true and righteous, I won't crumble. There is nothing in scripture that says the office of the Ancients will terminate the day the thousand years end."

"So, then, this meeting is final," said Moses. "You will not hear from us again on this matter. You will not be notified when it comes time for you to step forward on our behalf. You will reveal nothing of our agreement to anyone. You will represent us officially, but without any title or office. Our adversaries will try to make you look as though you are opposing our highest interests. We trust you to be steadfast and unmoved by our assailants. They will have a form of logic and righteousness but will be unwitting tools of the adversary."

"So this must mean that you are now preparing for the loosing of Satan?" Lev queried.

"Yes, it is not far off. Some of us have lived long enough in a world where his baneful influence was felt in almost every avenue of life. We often watched helplessly as he beguiled people into evil. He is such a loathsome creature, but God is going to use him once again before he is destroyed."

"I am glad for this information. I knew the thousand years was ending, and I thought it would be this fall. I do not need to know the exact date. It means little to me. No one can say they have not been informed about the way it would end. It is in very plain and understandable language. Those trying to get by without sufficient love for God or their fellow men only deceived themselves, certainly not Christ," said Lev. "By the way, after you leave office, where will you go? After listing your faithfulness, Paul in Hebrews 11:38 wrote, 'Of whom the world was not worthy.' I certainly agree that the world has never deserved such distinguished servants of the Lord. We got much better leadership than we deserved. Is the Lord possibly taking you to heaven and giving you a spiritual nature?"

"That is not for us to say, Lev. God has not told us where we are going or what is to become of us. The Lord is gracious and rewards those who serve Him with more than they deserve. Only veiled scriptures imply that something more for us may be possible."

Lev replied, "The Lord is wonderfully generous to those who demonstrate the kind of character that reflects His own. He highly exalted His son giving him 'all power in heaven and earth.' He rewarded the followers of Christ with immortality, and many of us feel you will be given a heavenly reward for faithfulness in your previous lifetime and for your tireless role managing earth's affairs now."

Moses added, "I often wondered about the promise to Abraham, 'And I will give unto thee, and thy seed after thee, the land wherein thou art a stranger, all the land of Canaan, for an everlasting possession' (Genesis 17:8). Abraham died without as much of a foot of the land and his sons through Isaac later came to possess it, but he never had it as an 'everlasting possession.' So God never fulfilled His promise to Abraham in his previous lifetime. Where will he go after his natural children receive the land 'after thee'?"

They talked long into the night. It was exciting exchanging ideas in a personal way with this great man of God. He was so wise and ruled himself with the same greatness that he had once ruled his people Israel. Finally, Lev said, "I must allow you to get some rest. The guest room is ready for you. You may want some tea before retiring."

No One Need Know of Our Visit

"No, thank you, Lev. Dinner was sufficient. I think I will turn in for the night. Remember that the purpose of our visit is to be shared with no one else, not even your family. You will not hear from us any further. I will leave in the morning immediately after breakfast. Shalom."

Lev tossed and turned throughout the night, having the assurance that the end of the Millennium was so near at hand.

His secret commission to represent the Ancients weighed heavily upon his thoughts. Such great moments as this were enough to make anyone tremble. He felt so unworthy. Also, the realization that the devil was soon to be freed to deceive all those that could be deceived was a troubling thought. Satan's dark and sinister involvement in earth's affairs was indeed frightening. The world had been free of his influence for so long! Lev remembered the old world when Satan's power was so pervasive. Evil predominated everywhere. The righteous suffered, and evil was on the throne.

Finally, as Lev was lifting his heart in prayer to thank Christ for being in charge of whatever experiences the future might bring, he peacefully drifted to sleep.

Lev awakened early, hearing Moses stirring about. He quickly arose and showered and soon had hot tea ready for his honored guest. Moses greeted him.

"Shalom, Lev. I cannot stay for your chapel meeting. There would be too many questions asked. I shall slip away quietly."

Moses spoke directly to matters and with focused thought. He said, "I need to tell you that you have been given a very difficult assignment. You are going to be in the line of fire, as it were. At first people will talk kindly to you, but then they will challenge your right to represent us. If we represented ourselves directly, they would back off because they know our authority and would not be so bold. By not meeting us face to face, they will be more fearless."

"I guess this will give some greater courage in pressing for their demands," Lev said. "Thank you for your insights, Moses. I know Satan is a wily foe. He has always been a master at making wrong appear right and right appear wrong."

"You are not ignorant of his tactics," Moses said. "Satan has been in isolation for a long time, and he must have refined his strategies so they will have tremendous appeal. Never underestimate the enemy. He will make you appear as the one standing in the way of righteousness and progress. He is good at what he does, make no mistake about it."

"Truth is easier to defend even if it is unpopular," replied Lev. "I only hope I am able to represent you as you deserve. I know I cannot outwit Satan. He is superior to men in his capabilities and will make me look very inadequate."

"Do not worry about appearances," Moses said. "Satan will do what is needed to appeal to the hidden ambitions within the hearts of the people. His ways have to look right in order to get people worked up to demand change. If you appear backward in representing us, that will be all right. It will only be an appearance and not the reality. Satan will succeed in deceiving many. God has foreseen all of this. You must remember that Satan is unwillingly and unwittingly helping God remove those unworthy of eternal life. Yes, some will have passed for 'sheep' and think they will be among those whom Jesus says, 'Blessed are they that do his commandments, that they may have right to the tree of life' (Revelation 22:14). "

"I understand," said Lev. "Adam and Eve had this kingdom when they remained obedient to God. When they sinned, they lost the kingdom and also life. The same end will follow those who join Satan's rebellion."

Moses Departs

They talked through breakfast and then Moses made haste to depart. "Shalom, Lev. Remember this visit is confidential as is your future assignment."

Moses' aircraft rose gently and soon disappeared in a cloud. Lev stood staring after the craft. He felt a solemn trust had been laid upon him and hastened into his house to pray about this meeting and his awesome responsibility. The Lord alone would give him the grace and wisdom for this task.

*"And before him shall be gathered all nations:
and he shall separate them one from another,
as a shepherd divideth his sheep from the goats"
(Matthew 25:32).*

Chapter Ten

The fall of the year had come with earth's usual splendor, but Lev knew this autumn would be different from any other. He was saddened by the prospects of what he knew must soon transpire. He awakened early one day, sensing that something was going to change. There was a chill in the early morning air. It seemed the birds stopped singing all at once and a hushed silence hung over the earth. The time had come for the Lord to separate the "sheep" from the "goats." Yet no voice had spoken.

Lev heard his instruction center turn on. That was strange, for he remembered quite clearly turning it off before retiring last night. It came on all by itself. No picture was on the screen, but the voice he heard was awesome and commanding. Could it be Christ himself speaking? He found himself trembling and hastened to find a chair. Yes, the voice was undoubtedly that of our Lord. He simply stated that he must now make known the results of his reign. Starting this day the trial period of mankind was completed, and the time of rewards and punishments would follow. Just as suddenly, the voice stopped speaking. An eerie silence followed. Soon Lev's phone started ringing. A panicked neighbor called to ask him if he had heard the voice.

"Yes, I did. This must be the end of Christ's reign. It was clearly the voice of our Lord speaking."

"I know," the neighbor said shakily. "That was no human voice. What shall we do?"

"The time for doing is past," Lev replied. "We will either be declared fit to inherit the kingdom of earth or unfit. Nothing we do now can change the judgment for us or against us."

"I am frightened," his neighbor said.

"I don't think we could help but feel that way. That voice once raised the dead, and it is a voice that commands our entire attention," Lev replied. "But we should not be afraid. The one who spoke has done more for humanity than anyone. We all owe our life to him."

The neighbor exhaled suddenly as if he had been holding his breath. "Yes, thanks for reminding me of that fact, Lev. I guess I will just listen for more information. Shalom."

Even those who were outdoors had heard the voice and heard very clearly what was said. It was not natural in any way. Everything stopped that day. There was a complete blackout of all programming. Everyone waited in anticipation for further information, but none was forthcoming that day. After about an hour the regular programs came back and carried the news of Christ's announcement.

The world became very sober as everyone waited for some further development. It was a time of intense soul searching.

Would Christ's Love Save Them?

The passing hours were filled with tension. Those who had been confident that Christ's love would save them were a little less so. The reckoning was at hand and only those who had done well would hear "Well done" from their Master.

Fortunately most people had done well and were caring and generous in giving of themselves to others. There had been an amazing amount of love demonstrated throughout the centuries of regeneration. Now, of course, there were many people with serious concerns. The past was not to be retrieved. There was no redemption from the past omissions. Still the idea persisted that as long as they were upstanding people, a loving Savior would not let them go.

The next morning the same thing happened. All information centers lit up again, and Christ declared all industry would close down operations for one week. Everyone traveling was to return home as soon as possible. It was a time for families to gather together. No business, however important, was exempt. Even air services would close down when everyone was home. Something profound was to take place, and everyone was in a very grave mood.

Lev was grateful that matters were not in human hands. Christ, the righteous Judge, would render each verdict. He would not judge by the seeing of the eye or the hearing of the ear, for he knew the thoughts and hearts of men. There was no possibility that he might err in judgment, and hence there would be no appeal from his verdict. Only those judged worthy to inherit the kingdom lost by Adam and Eve would become heirs of the kingdom. Under this arrangement there seemed to be a quiet resignation among men to accept the final verdict with grace and candor.

Christ did not speak again for several days. The Ancients were silent, also. It was crystal clear the final decisions were to be made by the infinite Judge, Christ. The Ancients had done everything that could have been done to awaken everyone to their privileges and responsibilities, and now there was nothing to be done that would change anyone's fate.

Lev spent the time with his family members. Jake, his brother, who had always been busy, found his vacation very relaxing. He told Lev, "I have never been this relaxed since I can remember. Let's spend a day together with the Aron family. We are all nearby so it won't take us away from home. We can keep our ears tuned for any further messages from our King."

"Sounds good to me," Lev replied. "We could have a little family reunion."

"Great! I'll tell Rachel, and Annie and maybe I'll bake some desserts. We can meet at Hannah's place tomorrow," Jake affirmed.

"Good idea," said Lev. "Allon is home and was planning to be with Grandma Aron anyway. I'll call Rebekah."

The next day brought no further news from the King. The Aron family gathered the next day with special joy to have all the immediate family members together. Grandma and Grandpa were beaming as their children gathered. Allon said, "Maybe some day we can have a family tree convention."

Lev responded, "If you're not careful that would include Adam and Eve."

"We would have to make it smaller than that, Dad," Allon said with a grin.

Annie laughed, "We'll have eternity to work out the details. I'm not going to worry about that now."

Queen for a Day

"Welcome, my beloved family!" Hannah was all smiles. "I understand that I am to be the queen for today. The girls and Jake have brought all the goodies, and Lev is taking care of all salads and veggies. That leaves Allon to do the dishes."

Ariel grinned, "I guess that makes me king for the day! I thought I would be assigned to the dishes and clean up detail."

"Oh, Grandpa, we wouldn't let you do that!" Annie said, hugging him. "You deserve being king for a day. You are the most wonderful grandfather ever! We rejoice to serve you today. We owe you so very much that we could never repay you and Grandma."

"Annie, you must tell us more about South America," Ariel queried.

"I'm afraid I don't have any more exciting tales about being deserted in the jungles and having to find my way home alone through the scary wilds. South America is so different than when I first went there. Back then they had witch doctors and voodoo. The changes have been dramatic! Poverty and ignorance disappeared very quickly. As soon as the trees of life started producing fruit, you could see a huge difference. After a few years, the former witch doctors were managing the factories efficiently, and soon we had research centers and made marvelous discoveries. The people had no problem forsaking their dark past for the intellectual present. They devoured all the information they could get their hands on."

"How has it changed since you wandered alone in the jungles?" asked Rebekah.

"In every way it is more hospitable now. The densest foliage is gone and today's jungle is very friendly. About every square mile has a place where people can stay overnight or rest during the day. There is a grove of trees of life at each pavilion with ample provisions for every human comfort. One can walk safely day or night in the former jungles, which are still heavily wooded, but free of ticks, mosquitoes and all the insects that used to prey on us. Animals are tame and friendly, and they love being with people. It is really a beautiful paradise now. Instead of hunting the animals for food, the managers are controlling their reproduction, allowing only so many animals for a given area. People enjoy watching the animals in their natural settings and are learning more about them all the time."

Lev said, "I would like to visit there sometime. It sounds wonderful!"

"Oh, it is, Uncle Lev! Animals have come to trust human kindness. They used to drink dirty river water, but we have provided them fresh drinking water, cold and pure, and they love it. They like the abundant protein grass and eat their fill without having to hunt for food. If we allowed them to enter the pavilions, they would probably enjoy the air conditioning also. We haven't gone that far in pampering them yet."

"It sounds as though South America has become an Edenic animal paradise," Ariel asserted.

"It has, Grandpa!" Annie exclaimed. "To appreciate all the changes you have to remember its dark past. The people were ignorant and exploited by industrialized nations. Their land was confiscated by wealthier nations who stole their natural resources. They had disease, starvation and poverty to contend with, along with the constant fear of losing their land and way of life. When I came among them they gradually learned to trust me, and from then on I have been treated as a queen. At times, the lavish care they showered on me was embarrassing. I went there to sacrifice on their behalf, but they didn't think I should be working. I had to insist on it."

"You were a queen, Annie," Grandma lovingly added. "They felt the love that was in your heart, and they wanted to respond with love. It is wonderful the way love begets love in others."

Learning Accelerated

"It was funny to watch them starting to learn from their computer screens," Annie reminisced. "They wanted to learn so intensely that they asked endless questions. They were so backward at first that they needed extra tutoring to understand what was being said. I understood their plight, so I spent most of my time helping them deal with the new technology. Within a few months, the learning curve shortened. Soon they could easily grasp the lessons and then the learning accelerated beyond all my expectations. It was amazing to see people turn into intellectual giants in a relatively short time."

Jake said, "Yes, Annie, those two people you sent to our science center were certainly helpful. They became very productive and had marvelous ideas. We taught them to turn the ideas into real products. After several years working with us they went back and established a science center in their own country and, needless to say, it has been a shining light in South America."

"The savagery of the jungles has become a peace zone with animals and mankind dwelling together in harmony and love. Not only are the people glowingly radiant, but also all the animals are friendly and peaceful. We used to see such unpleasant scenes around us—horrifying genocide and animals preying upon each other. Most of the world closed its eyes to the savagery of that time. It was accepted by many as the theory of 'the survival of the fittest.' The poor people languished, hoping for a better time. And, thank God, that day finally came."

"Yes, Annie, and now we are going to remove every trace of selfishness from the earth," Lev added. "Those who have not learned to love in the highest sense are about to be removed from the earth. It may seem hard and cold, but it is really a further demonstration of God's mercy. Death won't be painful to those who must receive it, and they would not have been happy living frustrated for eternity."

Ariel nodded, "And yet another purge must transpire before the earth is purified of the toxins of sin. Satan will soon be loosed to call those with hidden ambitions, who are waiting to be engaged in his plans. He will know those who have such desires. Some people seem to be good, generous, and giving, but hidden in their hearts is a wish for prominence. They can pass the test of generosity to others, but they are possessed by desires of power over others. Satan will have a siren song that will appeal to them. The Ancients were the visible source of authority, but they were only following the higher orders of Christ and his followers."

"We've been governed so well for so long that we assume perfect government is automatically our heritage. The credit all goes to Christ, who has ruled without making a single mistake in his long reign. Perfect wisdom with perfect knowledge has made everything move flawlessly," replied Lev. "It looks easier to do than it is. How foolish to assume that we could do as well, given the opportunity. That is a very serious mistake."

The discussion continued until Lev started preparing lunch. Quickly everyone turned to getting ready for a sumptuous feast. The salads were soon ready and the vegetables were steaming. Cakes and delicacies were prepared ahead of time. Soon Hannah rang her dinner bell.

No Wrinkled Brows

As they sat down together, there was a sense of joy and fulfillment. There were no wrinkled brows worrying if this might be their last gathering. However, not all families were enjoying this holiday equally. In some families there were gnawing doubts, realizing that perhaps some of their members had lost many opportunities to serve their fellow men.

After their sumptuous repast, Allon spoke of his experiences in what had been formerly Ghana, Africa. "I have really enjoyed my work in Ghana. When I arrived there, I felt my assignment was larger than my ability. But the people were so welcoming that soon I lost my fears and my longing for home. They had been more advanced than some of the warring factions in Africa and, consequently, were more ready for the rule of Christ. They were enthusiastic about learning and building. They worked tirelessly by day and studied long hours into the night, so we had an eager team that was ready to accomplish its goals." Allon leaned back in his chair and ran his fingers through his blond hair before continuing.

"There was no resentment shown toward me or my position at any time. And no attempts to sabotage our efforts as Dad experienced in Germany. People weren't so "position conscious" — no one wanted to replace me. Most of our problems were technical in nature, and we worked as a team to solve them. I must admit, they came up with many of the solutions. They were very intelligent and daily becoming more so. All my fears of failure melted away in that friendly atmosphere.

"When my initial assignment was finished, I thought I would be sent elsewhere, but the people insisted that the Ancients keep me there. I soon became one of them. I grew in admiration of them daily. They are wonderful people with an enormous capacity for worship. They are always singing hymns of praise while they work. And you should hear the harmonies they create, almost without thinking! Maybe that is why we were so successful in our projects. As Uncle Jake knows, we came up with some stunning breakthroughs in science, so we weren't just manufacturing products but becoming innovators of many things for the advancement of mankind."

The family discussion lasted into the late afternoon. After a light supper to finish up all the food, the happy company drifted homeward for the evening. Yet, it was not as other days for a certain foreboding still hung over them, the knowledge that the "sheep" would soon be separated from the "goats." It was not a time of rejoicing, but of soul searching. Even if one were secure that he or she had done well, it was hard to realize that some with whom they had shared experiences would no longer be with them.

"Come, Ye Blessed of My Father"

The following morning, all media transmissions were closed to normal exchanges. Everyone who had passed the test as a faithful "sheep" was called on his own receiver. The phone lines became overloaded as people were congratulating one another on graduation day. Those who passed the test were rejoicing with those they loved. Those who found they were omitted from the "sheep" list were very solemn. The decisions affected many families, for some members had been found worthy while others were not mentioned, leaving a pall of sorrow to be endured.

The sheer magnitude of the events that day was beyond anyone's ability to digest. Lev found himself torn between happiness, knowing that his family was in the "sheep" category, and sadness for those whom he knew were not. He spent the day in quiet contemplation wishing to learn everything he could from this experience. While he felt sorrow for those who did not make it, he also realized the world could not endure having people who failed in their devotion to God.

It was not as though the events of the day were not foreknown. Everything had been clearly written in a way that no one could fail to understand. Reading it over again today only made the drama more impressive. The "sheep" had to be separated from the "goats." Who separated them? They separated themselves. Their works demonstrated their heart condition. A long time had been involved, so if anyone failed some opportunities, there would be plenty of other opportunities to redeem themselves.

Those Not Included in the "Sheep" Were Apprehensive

No one had been designated a "goat" yet, but there were plenty of apprehensive people waiting for the other shoe to drop. Everyone thought the morrow would bring this news, but it did not. There wasn't great jubilation among the "sheep" class for this very reason. Out of concern for the unhappy plight of their brethren, the "sheep" class were very subdued.

Those who had not been identified as "sheep" were claiming, "Death isn't so bad after all. We all know what death is like, and none have complained about the years they were dead. As a matter of fact, many complained that they had been brought back to life without their consent. We came into this world without choice originally, and so it has been in the regeneration."

Lev realized that when it came to death, unless one was suffering in pain, no one really wanted it. Life was beautiful—it was God's gift. He had no pleasure in anyone's death and invited all to choose life that they might live.

The "goats" had unconsciously tried to dictate the terms of their acceptance to Christ. They misjudged the standard, thinking that by changing from the evil of their past ways it would surely make them acceptable now. Proverbs 16:25 said, "There is a way that seemeth right unto a man, but the end thereof [are] the ways of death." The time for following perceptions and feelings was at an end. Every man's work was going to be made manifest with unerring accuracy. The mask worn by the heart would soon be taken off for all to see.

*"Then shall they also answer him, saying,
Lord, when saw we thee an hungered, or athirst, or a stranger,
or naked, or sick, or in prison, and did not minister unto thee?
Then shall he answer them, saying, Verily I say unto you,
inasmuch as ye did [it] not to one of the least of these,
ye did [it] not to me.
And these shall go away into everlasting punishment:
but the righteous into life eternal"
(Matthew 25:44-46).*

Chapter Eleven

It was a cool autumn day when Lev awakened. The information center lit up and spoke in that unmistakable voice of Christ. Every communication channel carried the same message. Names of persons by families, by nations, and by sequence of birth listed the "goats." The complete listing was available for everyone to search out this information. No one could fail to know his personal standing. It was clearly stated.

Lev sat stunned by what he heard. He decided he would not search the list, and he would learn the news soon enough as different ones voiced their dismay. He remembered talking to many who smugly felt that they were secure because of their righteousness. They had felt strongly that only the very wicked would perish, and they knew they were not wicked.

Now was not the time to remind them. The die was cast and no further discussion was necessary. The judgment received was just and righteous altogether. Yes, one felt pain for the condemned. It was not easy to see one's fellow members of the human race being terminated. They had all shared moments together in life, and they were sweet moments. Yet, this was not sufficient to justify their existence, either. To mourn their fate would be a reflection upon Christ's verdict and that would be wrong. Yet, one did not want to be cold and uncaring. Families were being separated, which was always painful.

While Lev was in deep thought, the phone rang. Thinking it was a family member, he answered, "Shalom."

"Shalom, Lev—this is Johan Felbur, who stands condemned today. I just wanted to call you, hoping you remember me as one of your stout opponents on several occasions."

"Yes, Johan, I remember you very well, and I remember you chose to differ with me on several occasions. I hope you have no bad feelings for anything I may have said."

"No, Lev, I don't. You were right and I was wrong. I really never believed I would receive the judgment I did. Not that I feel it is unjustified. It is completely fair. I am ready to leave this world without a whimper. There is a certain peace in knowing that it is all over for me. It is not as though I do not know what death is like. I know how it was before I was born, and I know how it was when I was dead. I slept in peace. There was no pleasure in the grave, but no suffering either. I do not fear death and, at times, I have had a death wish. Not that life was unpleasant during the reign of the King, although sometimes I felt very frustrated. I am afraid I drank from the cup of pleasure too deeply to consider the needs of others. So, why am I calling you?"

"Johan, that saves me from asking the question."

"Lev, though we locked horns on some issues, I have always admired you. Some thought you were a smooth operator trying to get ahead in one way or another, but I always knew you were a genuine lover of people. I even thought several times I would like to be like you. I only wish now that I had tried harder."

The Past Cannot Be Changed

"I wish, Johan, that there was something I could do to bring some comfort to you. There is nothing I can say really. I only wish I had been more persuasive in my discussions with you. We cannot change the past."

"Lev, I know you were always fair with me. I didn't call you to tell you my troubles. I called to say I defended a wrong position. I know that you were right."

"Then why didn't you listen?"

"Because I'm too headstrong, I guess, Lev."

"You are paying a high price for being headstrong, Johan."

"I know, but this is the way I have chosen. Shalom, Lev."

Lev felt tears coming to his eyes when Johan hung up.

The phone rang again, only this time Rebekah came on with a voice betraying her tears. "Oh, Lev, I just heard from my childhood girlfriend, Aviva Volefski. She called to say 'goodbye.' She remembered me after all these years because I was the only friend who reproved her for doing certain things. The other girls reinforced the rude manner in which she treated the boy who deserted her."

"She had a long time to remedy her actions, I would think," Lev interjected.

"Yes, I know. Somehow she was never concerned with her actions as long as she got immediate results that pleased her. Now looking back, she realizes her lack of real virtue. It is too late for her to turn the corner now, but she wanted to tell me that many times in her life she had reflected on my example and knew I was doing the right thing. Unfortunately, she never decided to incorporate virtue before her own pleasure."

Lev responded, "I suspect there are many reflecting on where they went wrong along the way. As long as righteousness was rewarded, they managed to do well and passed for noble people outwardly. The difference is that some people loved God and their fellows in a genuine manner, and they showed it in their willingness to sacrifice for others."

No sooner had Rebekah hung up than Lev heard his phone ringing again. "Shalom, this is Lev speaking."

A Call from One Who Comes Up Short

"How does it feel to be a winner?" a voice asked.

"To whom am I speaking?" Lev inquired.

"Does it matter?" the caller said roughly.

"Yes, it matters to me," Lev said. "I like to know to whom I am speaking, if you don't mind."

"Apparently you are speaking to a loser," was the reply.

"Am I in anyway to blame for your being a loser?" Lev asked.

"I can't rightly say that you are."

"Then why are you calling me?" Lev replied.

"You don't remember me, but my name is Orville Summers."

"Thank you for the courtesy of your name, Orville. How may I be of assistance?"

"How does it feel to be on top of the world?" Orville said with some irony in his voice.

"All I can tell you is that I have a deep feeling of regret in my heart for many today that received the bad news. I have tried in all my contacts throughout the age to prevent this from happening to people, but it wasn't enough. What can I do for you now?"

"I remember you as one of those people who always seemed righteous in an extreme sense. I heard you in several discussion groups and you seemed kind of squeaky clean to me. Not that I am a revolutionist or wanted to tear down the establishment, but I came from a more permissive background. I thought you wanted people to be regimented in some kind of benevolent society, with everyone marching in lockstep. That wasn't for me. Now the day of truth has come, and I've come up on the short side."

"I came through pretty rough circumstances, too, Orville. I had a Jewish background, but I wasn't religious and lived a worldly life like most people. I served in the defense of Israel during Armageddon and died the first day defending Jerusalem. I did not live to see how the Lord fought for His people the second day. I fought bitterly, for we were outnumbered and outgunned. I remember dying. When I awakened from the dead, I still was a rebel of sorts, but truth was hard to resist. I soon found that I was the one who had to change. So I am surprised you found it odd that I should be squeaky clean."

"I thought you had some ulterior motive trying to create good impressions. I thought it was mostly a front. Frankly, I thought your name would appear with mine in the 'goat' column. This comes as a shock to me, Lev."

"I am sorry you misjudged me. That is easy to do when you can't read someone's heart. How is it that you didn't read your own heart and had to wait for Christ to read it for you, Orville?"

Too Busy Reading the Hearts of Others

"I guess I was too busy reading the hearts of others and was not looking into my own. That is where I went wrong, Lev."

"I am sorry you waited until now to learn what was crystal clear centuries earlier."

"Oh, don't feel bad on my account, Lev. Truthfully, I often wished that Christ had left me to sleep on in peace. This is for the best. I really don't belong in a world of love. I'm probably better off where I can't darken anyone's doorstep anymore. Shalom, Lev."

Lev felt a lump in his throat when he hung up. How would Orville's mother or father feel, or perhaps his children or other loved ones? This was not going to be easy. At least when people died the first time there was hope of a resurrection from the dead, but now it was forever. Attaining everlasting life was turning out to be a real challenge. Those who felt no need to reach higher were finding themselves not acceptable to Christ. Those who received the grace of salvation in Christ were indeed delivered from the original judgment standing against them. But failing to go on to perfect love for God and man, these had received the grace of Christ in vain.

Soon the phone rang again. "Shalom, this is Brian Heindlemann. Maybe you remember me from way back when you came to our plant in Germany?"

"Yes, you were one of the engineers who was unhappy with my management style. May I ask how you made out in the separation process?" asked Lev.

"Thanks to your good example, I am at Christ's right hand. I wanted to thank you, Lev, for your shining example. You know, I was hostile to you at first, but you were a hard person to dislike. It took me about a week to change my mind about you. You not only had better ideas, but your complete honesty in working with our department proved your worth. You made us feel like we generated the ideas. You gave us all the credit when it really belonged to you. I learned from your example and decided I was going to chart a different course in life. Thank you, Lev."

"Brian, thank you for the compliment. I found that love really works. If you cannot win people over with love, no other way works better. You have to persevere long enough to show them that you love them. Jesus proved that in his life and death. One lone, solitary life influenced mankind more than all the armies of the nations. He did it with love and changed the world."

"I had imbibed the world's spirit and had no wish to change. I was a smug believer in trying to be first and best. I'm afraid if I had continued in that path, I might be calling you to say 'good-bye.' Anyway, I wanted to take this occasion to thank you for showing me a better way, actually the only way—the way of love. It changed my attitude and my direction of living."

"Thank you for your very kind words, Brian. Little did I know that I was able to make a believer out of you! Shalom."

The day passed with many different contacts, mostly from those who knew they had failed. Then there were also calls from those who told Lev of his inspiring example that helped change the direction of their thinking. As the day closed, he was torn between the bad news and the good. No information had been given as to when or how the "goats" would depart. No funeral arrangements were to be made, so it seemed the "goats" would depart in the same miraculous manner that they came into the world the second time.

Amazing Calm

When the next morning came, there were no announcements. This gave another day for those departing to say farewell. Emotions were running high, but acquiescence to Christ's authority was also felt. It was not a decision that could be appealed. There was amazing calm and acceptance after Christ declared his reason for rejecting the "goats."

Would Christ announce a time for the "goats" to be taken or would it happen in a moment without foreknowledge? They were certain of death, but uncertain as to when it would overtake them. Some had previously died in infancy, some in youth and others in old age. Death came when it came, whether one was prepared for it or not. Maybe it would be a kindness to take the "goats" instantaneously with no pain—a peaceful passing into a lasting rest.

And so it was. The following night saw a miraculous disappearance of the goats. There was no need for funerals—the goats simply disappeared. Their passing was not to be mourned nor memorials erected to their memory. A quiet peace came over the earth, for those with flawed characters were quietly and justly removed. They would not have been capable of enjoying eternity lacking in perfect love. Yet, it was a sober time for earth's population. There was the realization that character was necessary to enjoy God's gift of life. Profession void of works was hollow, and only such that measured up to the standard of perfect love passed the test.

Serenity settled in by the end of the week of separation. Activities began as life as usual returned to normal. Lev found himself girding for another challenge. The world lost those whose sin was that of "omission," but now the final time of testing would be facing them—a time when Satan would be loosed from his prison. His nefarious influence would be felt, and some would fall under its lure. If he was subtle in swaying Eve to sin, he had a long time to perfect his new approach. He would make it seem the right thing to do.

Moses had forewarned Lev, so he was wondering how soon Satan's influence would be felt. The scripture was plain—"And when the thousand years are expired, Satan shall be loosed out of his prison, and shall go out to deceive the nations which are in the four quarters of the earth, Gog and Magog, to gather them together to battle: the number of whom [is] as the sand of the sea" (Revelation 20:7, 8). It was these verses that were constantly on his mind. When everyone was relaxing, there would be trouble from an evil source to come. Lev knew the temptation would appear innocently with noble pretensions.

When Satan was loosed, his influence would be in the air they breathed. If anyone wanted to express himself, Satan would be the most sympathetic audience. People who had tasted power once before might remember its sweetness and be enticed to seek it again. Those who had performed passively and who overlooked opportunities to serve others had now been eliminated, but those remaining were full of zeal. Zeal was beautiful when selfless, but it was dangerous when rooted in latent ambition. It was the desire to be wise as gods that temptcd Eve to disobey. Yes, she thought, how good it would be to enter worlds of light and knowledge in one swoop. The only knowledge she received was that of sin—shame, guilt, fear, grief, and anguish followed by death.

But today, everyone had the knowledge of good and evil, and the same deception would not work with those enlightened. Religion had been another tool of Satan. Religion spoke to man's higher qualities, but oddly enough those higher qualities were quickly forgotten in the quest to make religion a tool to dominate and control others. Some of the darkest pages of history covered the bloody and cruel deeds carried out in the name of religion. Religion as it was known in the past was not likely to be Satan's tool this time around.

Waiting for Satan's First Move

Lev thought he would wait for Satan's first move. Satan would have to find a spokesperson through whom he could operate, for no one would be foolish enough to march under his banner. Lev remembered Eve's resolve not to be beguiled again. She said she would not make a move until it had Christ's approval, no matter how appealing might be the presentation. Eternity was a long time and there was no reason to risk it by another mistake. She said, "Once was enough for me."

Lev was requested to make a quick trip to Sweden to review a normal technology function. While at the airport in Jerusalem, Lev noticed a crowd waiting for their plane. Usually they were seated comfortably waiting to board, but today it was different. The crowd was gathered around a handsome, very polished gentleman. He had angular features with a short, neatly-trimmed beard. Lev learned his name was August Hambers. Lev listened to the man and thought he was hearing the footsteps of Satan.

"It seems to me that we must be getting close to the day when the Ancients will be stepping out of office," August declared.

A petite woman agreed. "But I haven't heard of any preparations. You would think they would make some sort of announcement, wouldn't you?"

Yet another woman spoke. "I think they should have been preparing someone for their jobs. Maybe some of us should go to Jerusalem and apply."

August spied Lev in the crowd. "Say, Mr. Aron," he called out, "what would you say to going to Jerusalem and speaking to the Ancients about giving us some information on their departure from office?"

Lev, startled by the sudden attention, answered his request. "I would always be honored to speak to them, Mr. Hambers, but I have never tried to influence their decisions or make any suggestions to them. They have a higher source to guide them, and they do not need my advice. Why would they need me when Christ is their wisdom?"

August frowned. "I think you are putting our concerns in a rather unflattering light, Mr. Aron. We all know the Ancients are under the authority of Christ. No one in their wildest imagination would suggest that they not follow his instructions. They have governed flawlessly and should be honored for that. No one is saying we should give them advice, but would you consider asking them their plans for the future so we could know the direction of things? There would not be the slightest insubordination in doing that, Mr. Aron, would there? They know you and might appreciate knowing of our desire for direction if the question comes from you."

"Mr. Hambers, I am content with conditions as they are and, therefore, I will not be the spokesperson for you. If you genuinely feel you must know more than is presently revealed, you are free to ask the Ancients yourself," said Lev.

"What danger can there be in asking a civilized question, Mr. Aron? Surely there is no harm in asking."

Information Not Revealed Belongs to the Ancients

"The harm may be in asking for some assurance of their continued leadership instead of trusting them to make known their plans in due time," Lev asserted. "I positively am not a candidate to approach the Ancients for this consideration. It is my opinion that neither you, Mr. Hambers, nor anybody else should be so bold as to ask them."

"I can see that there is no need to discuss this with you any further, Mr. Aron," August replied, rather irritated.

"Remember, there is no emergency necessitating our doing anything. Everything is running smoothly. No one is in danger. No one is hungry. No one is in pain. Why do you have such concern about the Ancients? We will have no trouble while they remain in power, and there will continue to be a pleasant and efficient government. What is your concern, Mr. Hambers?"

"You seem to misinterpret my good citizenship as some kind of insurrection, Mr. Aron," August replied.

"Why are you so concerned about when the Ancients leave administration? Obviously, they have not been told to leave or they would. You should really direct your concerns to Christ. The Ancients are still in power because he has left them there. Can you not see that?"

"Certainly I know they would not continue to serve in defiance of Christ's orders," August defensively answered. "But at some point mankind is going to have to manage earth's affairs. Is it treason to inquire what our responsibilities are going to be and to work with some kind of schedule?"

"You are borrowing a burden not laid upon you. Christ has always done things in an orderly manner. The Ancients are not going to leave in the middle of the night with everything in disarray. What *really* is your concern, Mr. Hambers?" Lev asked.

"We simply want to anticipate our responsibilities and prepare to accommodate them, Mr. Aron. What is wrong with that?" August inquired.

"You are implying that unless you do some ground work now, there is a danger that we will be left in chaos. The Ancients have anticipated all our needs up to now and will continue to do so without any meddling on our part. What is revealed belongs to us. What is not revealed belongs to Christ and God," answered Lev.

The crowd seemed extremely interested in the discussion. Some were agreeing with Lev and some were not sure of any position yet. This surprised Lev because most people were not usually excited about something that was not really an issue now — or was it? Some were sympathizing with August. He was eloquent and managed to parry every point that Lev made. This alarmed Lev. Everything could be questioned and even made to appear right. That seemed to be a script that had Satan's backing. Why was the crowd so animated by the discussion? A disquieting spirit seemed to be forming.

Opposed to the Idea

As his plane began boarding, Lev told August, "I do not think this will end our discussion. Be certain of one thing, Mr. Hambers, I am opposed to the whole idea."

"Have a good trip, Mr. Aron. You have a needless fear of reality. The beauty of this age is the free ability to reason and seek the right solutions. Your mind is set against my being a good citizen. You seem to imply something dark and sinister will come by our seeking some information. Shalom," said August as he left for another plane boarding for Africa.

Lev felt sure that this issue was not going away. He experienced a sense of dismay that he could not budge his opponent. August Hambers was a man with a mission, and he was not going to be dissuaded easily, if at all. Lev realized this could have been the first evidence that Satan was getting his team together. He shuddered that August would even think of offering him the role of being their spokesperson to the Ancients. That was uncanny and frightening. What did August mean by, "I won't try to engage you for this cause?" Was he organized to make an offer? Lev's mind was spinning.

By the following day, Lev returned home thinking that perhaps he had overreacted to the incident with August Hambers. Yet, why did August so readily offer a place in his scheme of things to Lev? Why would he pick Lev, a stranger in the crowd, to confront?

Lev remembered his last visit by Moses, and now he began to see he was being targeted as a part of the loyal opposition. Strangely, he did not feel as effective as he should have been. He prayed about the matter repeatedly, desiring spiritual help. Lev felt he could deal with August, but he did not feel as capable against Satan. Satan was a wily foe and much more experienced than he was. Lev placed the matter in the Lord's hands, praying for divine wisdom to compensate for his weakness against such a fierce adversary. Unless the Lord helped him, Lev knew he was no match for the devil.

Lev did not tell his family members, not even Rebekah, about his conversation with Moses, as promised. None of his family was to be told, but that did not stop the devil from seeking to enlist him. This frightened him. Apparently Satan had marked him as his quarry from the beginning. Did he know of his talk with Moses? The Ancients had not communicated with Satan. He was still in the "abyss" when Moses had approached Lev. Yet, Satan had singled him out, and this left him a little frightened. Lev never faced such a formidable foe before, and he knew this was going to be a severe battle before it was finished. It was likely that he was known for his previous record in representing the Ancients.

Lev did not want to disappoint the trust the Ancients had placed in him. He was not afraid for himself, but many people were in danger of being deceived. He wanted his trumpet to give a 'certain sound' so they could be prepared for the battle. Some would be deceived; he knew that, for the Scriptures foretold this. Lev wanted his arrows to go straight to the target.

"The fear of the Lord is a fountain of life"
(Proverbs 14:27).

Chapter Twelve

Time passed inconsequentially. Lev had almost forgotten about August Hambers. As far as he knew, he might not see August again for centuries. However, as he entered the chapel that morning for worship, there was August Hambers looking energetic and greeting everyone with enthusiasm. When the two met, August was as congenial as ever, but he did not seem particularly eager to approach Lev about anything.

When the singing started, August's rich baritone voice could be heard clearly above the others. He was called upon for prayer and offered a beautiful one. He seemed a happy worshiper, and everyone enjoyed his being there. August paid close attention to the speaker's presentation, and after the service he was busy shaking hands with as many people as he could reach before they filed out. Lev decided he would stay long enough to exchange pleasantries with August before departing. When Lev approached him, August was his charming self.

"What brings you to our area, August?" Lev inquired.

"I'm on my way to Jerusalem to visit some of the Ancients. I hope to see them tomorrow. That will be my first face-to-face meeting with any of them, so naturally I am rather excited."

"You are in for a real treat! They are graciousness personified. I have had the privilege of meeting with them many times, and I know you will find them more wonderful than your greatest expectations. They are not nearly as busy as they once were, so you should have an unhurried visit," Lev replied.

"Perhaps you would want to join me tomorrow, Lev?" August invited.

"No, thank you. That is kind of you, August, but I have no business with them now. I would not want to intrude on your personal mission."

"Oh, I am not going for a personal visit. Many people have requested this appointment, and at last they agreed to see us."

"Do you mean you will be part of a body of people, then?"

"Yes, it will be a small committee, but I think we represent the wishes of all the people."

"What favor is being requested, may I ask?"

"Simply the privilege of praise."

Lev raised an eyebrow. "You certainly seemed free to praise the Lord at worship today."

"Of course we are free to praise the Lord, Lev. That will not be our request, I assure you," August responded crisply.

"Then whom do you wish to praise?"

"We have decided we should have a special day to honor the Ancients for their superb performance in office and their untiring care and guidance that have served us all so very well."

At first Lev was taken aback and wondered if this was sincere but misguided thinking. He said, "They're not prepared to receive such acclaim, so don't be surprised if they turn your request down for making a special day of tribute to them."

"Why would they turn our request down? What harm could there be expressing gratitude for the services rendered from them?"

"If Christ wanted them to be specially recognized, August, he would order such a time and place. You are asking them to authorize their own day of recognition, and they will be reticent to do that."

"Why should they be embarrassed to receive a heartfelt 'thank you' for a job well done?"

"Well, August, I can only say that if I were in their place, I would not be receptive to the whole idea. Could it be that you want to remind them that their job is done and the time to leave office has come?"

"Why do you place the worst construction on our simple and pure desire to honor these noble servants of the Lord?" challenged August. "You do us a disservice by your insinuation, Lev."

"You certainly do not expect them to authorize such a request, do you?" Lev asked. "It sounds innocent enough, but why not do it when they declare their work finished? I think this is pushing the limits of good taste. I am certain they will not grant your request. However, you may try. I could be wrong. At any rate, I will have no part of this."

"Do you mean you will not join in honoring the Ancients? For one who has served under them, Lev, you seem rather ungrateful not wanting to pay them the honor due."

"I just think it would be more appropriate to wait until it is clear that their service is at an end. Anyway, their praise will come from Christ himself, and they will receive it gladly. Some may be loud in their praise of the Ancients who are wishing them to step aside," argued Lev.

"I am sorry that you won't join us, Lev. But you should not judge our motives."

"I have to be true to my convictions, August. I know in my heart I admire the Ancients as much as anyone, but I am not prepared to embarrass them. Will you let me know what their answer is?"

"Why should I?"

"Just as a courtesy. I want to know their reason for refusing, if you would be so kind."

"All right. They may be surprised to learn that there is a groundswell of praise awaiting them. You know, we have done nothing to show our gratitude to them. That's not right, is it, Lev?"

"Oh, there has been quiet praise ascending to God right along, August."

"That may be true in many spiritual matters. Waiting on the Lord is proper. However, in the matter of praise there is no rule that indicates we should wait to say, 'Thank you.' The Ancients have been serving people around the clock for centuries. How much longer should we wait to say, 'Thank you'?"

As August turned to depart, he said, "I am almost certain the Ancients will grant us airtime to arrange for this day of praise. However, Lev, I will call you to let you know their answer. Fair enough?"

"I will be waiting to hear from you one way or the other, August. Maybe I have misjudged the matter."

They departed with a firm handshake. August was scheduled to meet with the other members of his committee later that day in Jerusalem, where they would finalize their plans to present their "day of praise" idea to the Ancients.

Lev was pleased to know that August would inform him of the outcome of the meeting. He was anxious to know how the Ancients would handle it. He suspected the Ancients wouldn't be enthusiastic about the plan, but at the same time, they might have to make some concessions to an international committee requesting airtime.

Granted Airtime

August's carefully structured plan made no mention of the Ancients leaving office, so it seemed innocuous. Lev sensed that the desire to praise was really meant as a reminder that their stay in office was shortly to end. This could indirectly be connected with the desire of some to take over the management of earth's affairs. The end result remained to be seen.

At the end of the following day, true to his promise, August called him to report on the committee's meeting with the Ancients. From the tone of August's voice, Lev could tell there was a measure of disappointment.

August greeted him warmly. "Shalom, Lev. I am calling to fulfill my promise to you. The meeting was very cordial, and we were granted airtime as we requested."

"So you got permission for the day of praise, right?"

"Well, not in so many words. They wouldn't assign a special day as a holiday for their praise, because they said that would be a self-serving misuse of their authority. So that cripples our whole plan. If we announce a day of praise for the Ancient Worthies, it won't be a holiday. They also would not agree to participate in any way in the festivities or be available for interviews. They said that only Christ could authorize what we were seeking. Therefore, we have only the airtime and nothing more. It is a bitter disappointment, Lev. They will not even appear at any festivities in their honor. So how can we make a party in their honor without them?"

"Obviously, August, they do not want this. I can understand their position. They cannot authorize a day of praise in their honor, and they will not use their office to aggrandize themselves in any way."

"I am disappointed that our plans were so coolly received. They didn't even thank us for our good intentions in this matter. The committee was very discouraged. I don't know what we'll do," sighed August.

"You will look foolish if you go ahead without their endorsement, August. Yet how could they give it without appearing to be seeking praise?"

"We will go ahead with our plan, Lev. We were granted airtime, and we will take it. However, we will be forced to modify our goals somewhat."

"What was your plan, may I ask?"

"We will pay tribute to them and express appreciation for their tireless and brilliant performance in office. Would you be willing to join us, Lev?"

Lev sensed a strong desire for his cooperation. Perhaps this was why August shared so much information with him. Though Lev certainly shared veneration for the Ancients, he sensed the praise being raised was to legitimatize a hidden agenda. "No, I am sorry, I cannot join you, August. I will wait for the proper time to honor the Ancients. You are trying to do the right thing at the wrong time, it seems. It goes against my instincts and better judgment."

A Negative Response

"Well, so be it!" August's voice was showing his irritation with Lev. "We shall do just fine without you."

"Thank you anyway, for telling me the outcome of the meeting. You honored your word and I appreciate that. Shalom, August."

Lev knew they were going ahead with their plans even though frustrated with the original intent of having the Ancients' participation. He could not help feeling this was in some way calling attention to the fact that their tenure in office should be ending.

"The Day of Praise"

Lev did not have to wait long to learn how the day of praise would play out. The Praise Committee was given airtime with just two weeks' notice, so they could not make elaborate plans. They faced a lot of questioning in the process. Many had the same reservations as Lev and, consequently, the committee spent much of its time justifying its actions. However, no one could deny that the Ancients were worthy of praise.

The program started with a scenario of the conditions on the earth when the Ancients arrived. August was the narrator with his distinctive baritone voice. He presented the Ancients in a most dramatic setting. They appeared on the scene when the world had just experienced Armageddon at its darkest hour. Never had there been a more chaotic time on earth. Starvation and hunger were rampant, and violence made it impossible to regain any stable government. At such a hopeless moment, the new leadership appeared on earth and began the work of bringing peace and stability. Their appearance in Israel and in the Holy City of Jerusalem settled the international question that brought the world to Armageddon. Jerusalem was to be the city of "the Great King." It had become the undisputed capital of the whole earth.

The Ancients brought prosperity to Israel and to every nation that came under their authority. They astonished the world by bringing with them seeds from the trees of life, which brought rejuvenating potential to the human race. Those nations that yielded to their sovereignty were the first to experience the phenomenal healing and restorative qualities of the trees. Soon all nations looked to Israel and the healing accelerated.

Aside from the unparalleled benefits of the trees of life, the brilliant management of earth's resources ended poverty and friction among nations. There were no errors as every effort to build and plant turned the earth into a garden. No politics entered into the decision making and nothing was done except for the common good. Earth had never known such benign governance.

Besides physical prosperity, people were taught how to live in a righteous society. Those who would not learn righteousness were given only a hundred years before they expired. This was a necessary corrective process in a righteous world. The wealth of the world seemed to be limitless under their authority, and above all else, everyone shared equally in it.

The praise program was interspersed with music between the narratives. They had composed new songs of praise for the Ancient Worthies. All in all, it was a genuine tribute to these noble leaders and no fault could be found in what was said. However, as the program ended, Lev caught an undercurrent.

Praise with a Hint of Reproach

In closing the program, they mentioned how the world would have to adjust to taking responsibility for world governance when the Ancients left their tenure of office. Was the world prepared to continue the same quality of government without these great leaders? What preparations were being made to insure a flawless transition? The audience was left with the impression that nothing was being done to this end. This was a program that, although full of praise of the Ancients, also hinted at a weakness in failing to groom successors to their leadership.

Lev knew immediately that this whole program was designed to put pressure on the Ancients. These proponents of change had not forgotten the sweet taste of power. There was a desire to be seated in earth's ruling power, and it was being pushed under the guise of "praise" for the Ancients. How glad Lev was that he had resisted joining forces with them! He expected things would not stop here. Would the message serve as a siren song to those of the same mind as August and his committee? Lev detected Satan's opening wedge of rebellion.

The program, in fact, had its desired effect. It started to awaken latent yearnings for self-government. Lev began receiving calls from people who thought the program was timely, asking why there weren't preparations being made for a smooth transition of government when the Ancients left office. Lev was chided for his lack of enthusiasm for the praise given the Ancients and for failing to see the need for training people for a smooth transition.

Charlotte Mangis, his last caller, was especially critical of Lev for his failure to cooperate in sponsoring the program. Lev asked, "How did you know that I had declined, Charlotte?"

"August Hambers specifically mentioned that you and a few others who had been used heavily by the Ancients were approached to cooperate in giving praise to them and that you steadfastly refused," she said. "Is that true?"

"Yes, that is true," Lev admitted.

"How could you not join in such a lovely program of tribute to those who served us so faithfully?" she chided.

"I am sorry August forgot to tell you *why* I declined any part in that program," Lev interjected.

"Why should he? It is obvious that you were quick to take assignments that made you famous, but now you are slow to give the Ancients the praise they so justly deserve," she stated forcefully.

"Charlotte, I think August owed me the courtesy to give the reason I declined. After all, I had good reasons for declining. I resent your insinuation that I lacked appreciation for the Ancients. That is totally untrue."

Skewered for a Lack of Enthusiasm

"I am sorry if I have misjudged you, Lev, but I can't sympathize with your lack of enthusiasm," she snapped.

Lev found himself being judged and condemned without the opportunity to explain his reasons for refusing to join the program of praise. He sensed that people were becoming agitated in a way he had not seen for centuries. Satan was certainly busy stirring up passions. He sensed that while Charlotte had exceeded the bounds of propriety in demeaning him, she was so passionate in her convictions that it did not matter to her.

"Charlotte, you may arrive at any conclusion you choose. I know you think you are in the right and that I was very wrong in failing to join in the praise. But I told August precisely why I would not participate, and he should have told you my reasons. By failing to do that, he misrepresented my position. I do not have to declare my innocence to you," Lev said sadly.

"Lev, you must have been a lawyer in your previous life—one that managed to defend and exonerate the guilty," she quipped.

"You still have not asked my reasons for declining to join you. I see no reason for discussing the matter any further. Shalom," Lev said forthrightly.

Lev found himself in the center of the storm while being an innocent bystander. Satan was a fast operator, and he was trying to destroy Lev's credibility. However, Lev was not troubled by the insinuations and aspersions hurled at him. He knew he had done the correct thing. What a blessing that Moses had forewarned him! If the Ancients wished to put down this spurious movement of praise, they could have easily done so. Their silence gave August Hambers and his followers a lot of room to press on with their agenda.

The seeming sincerity with which Hambers had flooded the Ancients with praise led many into believing that their concerns for the future were valid. No one would suspect that they were pushing to have the Ancients leave office. They looked like genuine, loyal supporters. Lev appeared as a once-active servant, now turned indifferent to those who had placed great trust in him. No one had bothered to tell Lev's side of the story, and if told now, it would sound absurd.

Lev was willing to be cast in the role of an ungrateful servant. Being faithful did not require the praise of others. He knew that while they had given proper praise to the Ancients, it was to gain credibility in the eyes of the people seeking them to retire from office. The whole thing lacked sincerity and the "fear of the Lord."

"The fear of the Lord is clean"
(Psalms 19:9).

Chapter Thirteen

Lev continued to be assailed for turning down the opportunity to render praise to the Ancients. He found himself at the forefront of the criticism, but he knew he was only being used to draw attention away from the real issue. What did it matter if he didn't participate? Not everyone had joined in the praise that day, but he was being singled out. He had been cleverly set up so that his refusal to cooperate could be used against him.

It was unpleasant when the criticism came from people whom he did not know. He was taken back when some of his friends questioned his motives, while August Hambers was being acclaimed for his noble endeavors in crediting the Ancients with their magnificent work in the regeneration. No one seemed interested in an explanation for his failure to join the program.

But then when Rebekah began questioning him, Lev was quite disturbed.

"Now you, too, are questioning my decision? Are you going to be deceived by this August Hambers?"

"Why, Lev, I wasn't criticizing you. All I asked was the honest question that everyone has been asking. I know you have an answer, and I want to know what it is."

"You are the first person to ask my reasons. I told August, but he never once mentioned them to anyone. Now no one will listen to me, because they are all convinced it was my vanity standing in the way."

"Please, Lev. I know you must have valid reasons, so how about sharing your thoughts with me. I think it is time you confided in me."

Lev Refuses to Join the "Praise Movement"

"I could not join in that movement, because I sensed it was a subtle means of trying to get the Ancients out of office, and that is indeed the note it ended on. Everyone was so enamored with the splendid tribute given to the Ancients that they didn't consider the closing remarks. Remember Hambers said, 'the world would have to adjust to taking responsibility for world governance when they left their tenure of office. Was the world prepared to continue the same quality of government without these great leaders? What preparations are being made to insure a flawless transition?' That was a dark insinuation that the Ancients were derelict in their duty. Didn't you notice that, Rebekah?"

"Yes, now that you mention it, Lev, I did feel a chill at that statement."

"Most people felt it, but the warmth of praise given made them dismiss it immediately. I could not dismiss it, Rebekah. It was very inappropriate for them to finish on that note. Yet, that is exactly what some people wanted to hear. You know they cannot wait to fill the offices that are to be vacated someday. That is the whole reason they praised the Ancients. They wanted to tell them they appreciated the *past* services, but it is time for them to move on. That was the message they wanted me to endorse, and I could not do it!" Lev said emphatically.

"Oh my, how could I have been so short-sighted?" Rebekah was dismayed at herself. "Yes, I heard those very same words, but I dismissed them as a reminder that we wouldn't have the Ancients around forever. I should have been more aware of the implications. Yes, you are absolutely right, Lev. I am thankful that you didn't join them. That was an awful thing to say, now that I think of it."

"The 'Praise Movement' is the opening wedge for getting people to want the Ancients to step out of office. However, the Ancients cannot leave until Christ tells them to. What these good people are insinuating is that the Ancients should step down before Christ releases them. In reality, it is Christ they are pushing to do their bidding, and that is serious rebellion! Though Christ is no longer serving as Mediator between God and man, he still retains 'all power in heaven and earth.' They don't suspect it, I am sure, but they are being beguiled into resisting Christ's authority."

"How could I not have seen that?" declared Rebekah. "I'm so ashamed that I was swept up in the praise that August Hambers gave the Ancients that I overlooked the grave implications of what he said. I should have been more alert, especially now that I know Satan is loosed to deceive anyone he can."

"I can't let him get away with this unchallenged," said Lev. "I know I will sound like a sore loser trying to defend my lack of enthusiasm in gratitude to the Ancients."

"What will you do?"

Dander Rising

"I don't know yet, but for the sake of righteousness, I have to do something," Lev insisted. "I explained to August that the Ancients could not step out of office without Christ's permission, but he and his committee didn't want to hear that. I need to find a way to confront them publicly."

"I am so embarrassed to confess I was half-fooled by all of this," Rebekah said emphatically.

"If they had not approached me prior to the event, I might have been deceived, as well," Lev asserted. "We all felt the honor given to the Ancients was beautiful, and we let our guard down because of it."

Lev Seeks Airtime

Try as he would, Lev could not think of a way to enter the public arena to address this issue short of asking the Ancients for airtime. They had left word with the outer office that they would not allow airtime for any rebuttals. He knew they had their reasons and respected this answer.

The silence of the Ancients allowed the forces demanding change to gain strength. They could easily have answered the challenge to everyone's satisfaction, but they purposely chose to let the undercurrent gain momentum. Lev had to find another way to be heard. He learned that Hambers would be leading a delegation to Jerusalem to ask the Ancients for a tour of their offices. This had never been done before, but in the past it had been a very busy place. Now the work was minimal since society was stable and well structured. To Lev's amazement his group was welcomed to see their headquarters.

Lev planned to meet them at the airport with placards protesting the visitors' bold move to get their feet into the doors of Jerusalem's government. Lev called around to get help to carry on his protest. He knew hundreds of people who would gladly join such a protest, but he handpicked twenty-five to join him to greet August when he disembarked at Jerusalem. Some of the posters read, CHRIST HASN'T RELEASED THE ANCIENTS YET, HAVE YOU BEEN INVITED? — WHY ARE YOU HERE? — HAVE YOU BEEN ELECTED? — WE WANT THE ANCIENTS AS LONG AS CHRIST DOES — WE WANT THE ANCIENTS.

It felt strange to be organizing an old-fashioned protest, but that seemed the only way to start the discussion. Considerable numbers of people were aware of the undertones in August's closing remarks and desired to make a strong response. When August and members of his committee landed, Lev with his following was there to greet them.

At first, August was stunned to be greeted by protesters. He regained his composure saying to Lev and his followers, "Thank you for your concerns, but really we have been invited to come. You are insulting the guests of the Ancients."

Lev knew they had been welcomed to view their offices, but nothing more. All they would be looking at were rooms without an explanation of their functions. No questions would be fielded and no Ancient Worthy would be their host. Office staff members were to guide them on the tour, feed them, offer overnight lodging, and then take them to the airport early in the morning. They would learn nothing of operations and no vital information would be shared. They might learn who worked in the offices, but not what they did.

The delegation was sorely disappointed that no official was present to greet them. When they learned they would only be touring the offices, they were humiliated, especially realizing that no Ancient would be their guide. They were getting what they had requested, pure and simple. However, August was not one to be easily discouraged, and he was going to use the tour for publicity. He photographed many rooms and properly identified who worked in them. It did not matter that he was being ignored. He was going to use the occasion as though he had received the red carpet treatment. There were no news reporters to give them publicity, but that simply allowed them to create their own.

Visiting Empty Offices

The delegation spent the next day going through the countless offices, but gained little information as they went. August asked where the Ancients were, expressing his disappointment that they could not be present with the tour. They were told many had taken the day off, some were visiting other countries, and the rest were in session resolving some technical changes. August knew this was strange indeed, for usually Ancients were everywhere, but he wisely did not comment. The delegation knew they were being shunned.

The company of protestors was in front of the offices to greet them to August's dismay. He said, "Don't you think such protests are a return to the darkness of the past?"

"That's what we are trying to prevent," shouted a protester.

August turned red, but remained gracious, saying, "I cannot imagine why."

Another protester shouted, "Do you remember what it was like before the Ancients intervened in earth's affairs?"

August quickly responded, "I should protest also if anyone wanted to take us back to those dark ages, but what gives you that impression?"

"You do," several protesters shouted in unison.

"My word. You do have a low opinion of us."

"Nothing personal," replied Lev. "We just don't want the Ancients hurried out of office until their work is done."

"We have no power to remove them from office, you should know that," August responded.

"Thank goodness you don't, but you are certainly trying to make them appear as though they are hanging onto power with a desperate grip," said Lev.

"That's a most uncharitable view of our efforts to accord them the gratitude due them," August responded. "You are demeaning our noble motives as though we were here to drive these God-provided servants from office."

Lev's final statement was, "Come back when Christ releases the Ancients, and I promise we won't protest your visit then. Now is not the proper time or the place for your visit."

This confrontation was small and Lev felt, ineffective. To his surprise, in the international evening news the Ancients told of the protest that occurred yesterday at the airport and today in front of their offices. They told of the visit of August Hambers and the committee members touring the facilities of the Ancients. The report stated that due to unusual circumstances, no contact was made between the committee and the Ancient Worthies. However, they were given a tour of the normally busy offices. They even showed a picture of the protesters and the signs they carried. That got out the message that Lev was hoping for. The report even quoted Lev's final message to the committee without identifying him, saying, "Come back when Christ releases the Ancients, and I promise we won't protest your visit then. Now is not the proper time or place for your visit."

At last Lev knew in his heart that the Ancients had taken note of his efforts. No one else knew it, but to Lev it was apparent that Moses had authorized putting the protest on the international news that evening. Just a quick view of the scene at the airport effectively dealt with the controversy. Now the world was aware of both sides. Immediately, the effect was to polarize people on the issue of the Ancients. The overwhelming majority felt the protesters were right. However, those who felt the Ancients should make room for their replacements became more solidified and defended August and the committee of delegates.

Pressing for an Early Departure

It was blatantly obvious that Satan was at work now—not to everyone, but certainly to Lev and many who were not ignorant of the devil's devices. The devil was a wily foe, but those who remembered his methods would not have much trouble detecting something was not right in pressing for the Ancients to prepare for their exodus from office before Christ released them.

The effect of this episode was to awaken the people that trials and testings were about to escalate. The issues forced people to begin thinking about the aspects of transition. Yet, this was done in such a matter-of-fact way that no one could tell that the hand of the Ancients was involved. Only Lev remembered his visit with Moses, and now he realized he was going to be drawn into the fray. No one knew of his contact with Moses, probably not even the devil, because he had been in the "abyss" at the time. The Ancients had wisely refused Lev airtime, for that might have revealed that they favored him. The method they chose showed no partiality. It left August and his conspirators without any reproof from the Ancients, and this would only strengthen their hand. The Ancients could easily frustrate Satan's plans if they chose to, but they knew Satan was serving God's purpose in his spreading deception.

August called Lev when he reached home, "That was low of you, Lev, to photograph your protest against our visit."

"I can plead innocent to having it photographed, August. Our protesters had nothing to do with that, I assure you. I asked for permission to having airtime to state our case, but I was turned down. They would not even discuss it with me. You seem to have more clout with the Ancients than I have had. I assure you someone who just happened to be at the scene took the photo. I know there were no cameras from the press or television there."

August was silent for a minute and then said, "I'll take your word for it, Lev. I apologize for incriminating you. So, you say they wouldn't let you have airtime? That is encouraging to hear. Doesn't that show you, Lev, you are on the wrong side of the issue?"

"No, August, my mind has settled on the correctness of my position based on the principles involved. Nothing personal about you or your committee, I just believe that you are wrong. I respect your right to have another opinion, and I hope you respect mine."

"All right, that's fair, Lev. Thanks for confiding in me that the Ancients turned down your request for airtime. I am glad to see that they are neutral in the matter."

"That isn't neutral, giving you airtime and giving no one else a chance to refute your position."

"I see you don't take kindly to not being a favored son, Lev," August chuckled. "Maybe you'll change your mind and join us."

"Don't count on it, August. I'm not an opportunist."

"Shalom, Lev, you have made my day," August said in closing.

Lev knew that August was taking a lot of comfort in learning that the Ancients would not even consider his request. August mistakenly concluded that they favored his side.

However, after all was said, the protesters and their placards were on the news and the message was short but vital. What they saw moved most people. The enchantment of August's praise of the Ancients was lifted by his veiled suggestion that they should be cleaning out their offices to give way to their replacements. Most people were grateful to have such sterling leadership continue as long as possible. It was sacrilegious to hint at their removal.

"To the Pure All Things Are Pure"

Lev knew that to suppose that the Ancients were clinging to their offices in their lust for authority was outlandish. They had all gained a good report from God. They had been faithful under evil conditions on earth and, therefore, were entrusted with their current positions of power. They loved righteousness and hated iniquity. Satan could not be effective against such leadership, and that is why he needed a change in the governing body to work his deceptions.

Lev was content with the results of his first round with August and his followers. It was not a smashing victory, but at least it alerted people to the coming dangers. People were perfect now and not ignorant of sin and its consequences. However, for many centuries everything had been very simple, clearly right or clearly wrong, with no gray areas. Suddenly, the shield to temptation was removed. All were to endure the temptations of the adversary just as their first parents did, and the appetites for sin could be stronger than imagined. The time for the final test was coming quickly.

Everywhere people's telephones were busy as they discussed the Ancients' remaining in power. E-mails were heavily loaded with these concerns. Lev found himself praised and condemned by a deluge of calls. The topic had become a burning issue overnight. Even though no movement was actually being proposed to change anything, the very thought of the possibilities was causing apprehension.

August and his disciples of change had a lot of work ahead of them to sell their program to the people. Even those desiring change were nervous about anything that might appear as rebellion. They needed to be persuaded and assured that change was quite natural and would not affect the good life they were enjoying. People were more alert and not as easily deceived; however, intelligence alone would not save any from temptation. It was the discipline of the mind and heart that prevented people from tripping over the baited traps of Satan.

During the following months, Lev spent a lot of time on the phone being supported or assailed over his protest. He was the subject of debate everywhere. Everyone wondered why the Ancients remained silent when a word from them might easily have ceased all debate. The Ancients purposely stayed out of the discussion to allow the conflict to grow. This was going to be the final test upon mankind. No one would escape some form of confrontation and, therefore, must have a ready answer for his or her actions. One not only had to make right choices, but he also had to act decisively on those choices.

"I will keep my mouth with a bridle, while the wicked is before me" (Psalm 39:1).

Chapter Fourteen

Many months had passed since August and his company had made any public announcements. As a result, people were not discussing the timing of the change of government from the administration of the Ancients to self-rule by mankind at large. Up until now, Christ made all decisions and the Ancient Worthies carried them out. Since at some point, Christ would cease active administration of earth's affairs, a new organization called the Citizens for Self-Rule, headed by August Hambers, concluded that the new government of earth needed to be decentralized—something like state governments and a federal government on a worldwide basis.

The Citizens for Self-Rule developed a draft of a new government plan and sent it to the Ancients for approval, correction, and criticism. The Ancients immediately replied it was not in their province to address anything outside of their tenure in office. They said, "When we leave office, we will not have a word to say about how the new administration is to function. If those selected to replace us choose to continue our form of governance or choose to change, it will be their choice. Society will have both freedom of choice and also the responsibility for their choices."

Although August and his committee members were disappointed, they didn't feel rebuffed and were actually strengthened in their conviction that they were on the right track. At least they would have a workable plan ready to go when others were floundering. They decided, why not suggest the plan to the public at large in the form of periodicals? The people would be ready to accept and implement Hambers' ideas as soon as the Ancients left office. It only seemed like good citizenship, after all. That they couldn't duplicate a government controlled by Christ had not even entered into their thinking.

After reading the first edition, Lev decided not to comment on the overall plan. No provisions had been made for learning the history of decision-making processes or what was involved in them. There was no way to know the requirements until mankind sat down with the problems they faced. The plan the committee submitted was neither good nor bad, but was lacking in knowledge. It seemed apparent that the motive of August and his team was to place themselves in the position of leadership before any other possibilities could be considered.

Yet, many thought the plan was wonderful and certainly very democratic. Lev did not just dismiss their ideas without due consideration. Certainly at some point good planning would be of value. Yet the Ancients had not said that they would not have any information to pass on to their successors. Just because the Ancients were not making visible preparations for their successors did not justify anyone else organizing a government before they left office.

Seduction of the Masses Sought

As he had always done, Satan seemed to be trying to secure human puppets on the government level as the channel of his power. He was not interested in a small seduction of individuals, but in large rebellious masses. A movement that appeared innocent but ran ahead of divine instruction had all the earmarks of the deceptions of Satan. Lev wished he could discourage this obsession of taking over the government, but it seemed to be gaining momentum. With all the knowledge the people possessed of past history and their experience under the present arrangement, they felt adequately prepared to continue good government for the ages to come.

One evening there was a string concert of newly-written music for the community in a meadow near Lev's home. The night was warm and the stars twinkled brightly as all present were moved deeply by the sweet strains of violins and cellos.

When it was over, several neighbors gathered at a table where juices were being served. August Hambers' latest periodical had just come out that day, so it was on everyone's minds.

"It shouldn't be difficult to govern now," quipped James Osgood, one of August's admirers. "We have no crime and no money to tempt people into wrongdoing. No abuse of power would be tolerated. We are educated now, and, therefore, impervious to governmental corruption. If we find governmental needs increasing, we could modify it to our liking."

Lev listened carefully to James' arguments. They sounded good, but a bit smug. Conditions did not have to be grossly evil before sin could overtake people. Eve had been very pure and noble when she disobeyed.

Lev said, "James, you seem very relaxed. That amazes me. We should be very concerned about a change in government. You know Satan is loose."

James laughed. "I know he is loose, Lev, but no one is carrying placards praising Satan. He is facing perfect people now and will have difficulty finding anyone to follow him."

"He already has a band of sympathizers, James. I'm afraid before very long he will have a host of deluded people doing his bidding. He is a master of deception, and there are a lot of people that don't think they can be deceived."

"Oh, I know I couldn't be deceived, Lev. I hate everything Satan stands for," James asserted.

"Would you believe you are already repeating Satan's script?" Lev retorted.

"What?" asked James, rather affronted. "Lev, this is no joking matter."

"No one would knowingly volunteer to be a servant of Satan," Lev responded. "They are taken by guile just as Eve was—deceived as she was."

"So what is the deception?" James asked.

"You opened your conversation with me by using Satan's line. You assured me that good government would come easily. There was no danger of corruption. People were beyond that possibility. Yet at one time perfect people did sin, and they will do it again." Lev remarked.

"I know the Scriptures say Satan will deceive people into rebelling against the seat of authority. I have read that and I believe it. August is not being used as a tool of Satan. How could that be?" James was incredulous.

Obsessed With Replacement

"That is not for me to say. August wanted me to join with him in trying to prepare to take over the government when the Ancients stepped out of office. I refused to do it," remarked Lev.

"Why?"

"Because it wasn't the right time or the place to be talking about the Ancients leaving office before Christ released them. When they leave office, they will provide all necessary help and guidance to provide a smooth transition. August has been obsessed with taking over the government when they leave office, and that sounds like the devil's aspiration," said Lev.

"Oh, no, Lev. August and the committee were so profuse in their praise of the Ancients, they could not have just been saying that in flattery, could they?"

"Well, maybe not flattery. What they said was true, and it is not for me to judge their motives. However, it would also serve to clear them of suspicion in pushing so hard to get a head start on the incoming government. Why must they be obsessed with planning for replacements? The Ancients cannot leave until released from their duties by Christ. When they tell us they are leaving office and instruct mankind to make preparations for new leaders, then, and only then, it will be time to act. Under the guise of civil duty, August and his committee are making an attempt to get a hold on the office of the Ancients as soon as it is opened," declared Lev.

"I never would have guessed it. What you say is reasonable, Lev. I am going to give this some serious thought and prayer. I could be following someone right into rebellion. Thank you, Lev."

"Don't judge the motives of anyone, James, but do some hard thinking before you support any movement. Satan is perhaps more wily than before, for he has had a long time to make his plans," Lev reminded.

"That is good advice. I am going to discuss this with all my friends. I truly do not want to be beguiled by the devil," James affirmed.

"Remember one thing, James. The 'goats' were destroyed for what they did not do. Those destroyed when Satan is released are destroyed for what they do. The latter are activists, and in their frustration to take over the government they 'compassed the camp of the saints [Ancient Worthies] about' (Revelation 20:9)," Lev concluded. "You don't want to be in that crowd!"

"No, not on your life. Thanks, Lev. When I think about my relaxed attitude, it makes me tremble," James confided. "I am afraid I may have been too superficial in my thinking. Why don't you challenge August's committee on this matter? They are running a campaign without an opposing viewpoint."

"Oh, I don't want to oppose them at every turn. He is only trying to build credibility now, but if he gets serious about launching his government, I will certainly speak up," Lev asserted. "You know I organized the protesters when he came to Jerusalem with his entourage of followers. That hurt his progress to a considerable degree."

"Lev, I will be right there standing with you," James beamed.

"Good, James. I'll remember your promise," Lev added.

Hoodwinked

"Remember, James, pay more careful attention to what they say and *don't* say. People are failing to weigh the issues carefully. They remembered the praise heaped upon the Ancients, but they failed to notice the extravagant interest shown in taking over the offices that they hoped would be vacated soon," Lev noted. "Oh, and one thing more, James. I will need lots of help when the time is ripe—preferably from the various countries. How are you at recruiting?"

"I'm your man," he exclaimed. "I have connections all over the world. I am constantly traveling in my line of work. I service peripheral computer machines such as printers and information storage and retrieval systems. I have all kinds of contacts, and all the people I know can be as well informed as they want to be on any subject. I will pull together a staff of supporters that are fully enlightened on every move that August Hambers has ever made and also on his committee. Forming teams is my forte, Lev, and I think our meeting was providential. We will awaken some drowsy citizens of the peril being posed by premature adventure into government," James said with an awakened passion.

"Good, I will be counting on you. I needed some help, and I think you can provide me with the knowledgeable people I will need. They will have to be sharp and know what August and his committee are up to at every turn. I foresee his position evolving from praise of the Ancients to a final protest against them. An informed public will be the best defense. I fear he is being used by the Adversary without even knowing it," observed Lev.

"One thing more, James. Promise me that you won't jump the gun in any action on your own. I must be in charge of any activity," Lev insisted.

"Okay, we will only act on orders. We will be a very disciplined team, I assure you. I know you are a responsible and knowledgeable leader. I know your history, and it is full of faithful performance and impeccable integrity. The Ancients have used you extensively, and that is good enough for me. I am surprised that they haven't engaged you to represent them," James commented.

"I am sure they know best," Lev said, hoping not to answer any further questions.

"I know that," James observed.

"Good! I will give you two months to pull together our team of recruits."

"Yes, sir! I will go to work immediately and I promise I won't fail you. I am a good organizer, and I think I know the kind of people you need," James assured Lev.

Organizing to Meet the Threat

"I have a phone that no one can listen in on. My brother Jacob gave it to me awhile ago. He is into the latest technologies. I can see if he will give you one as well. That way we can talk and no one can hear what is going on. Give me your address and phone number, and I'll get it to you in a day or two. One more thing, don't mention my name. Let your friends answer to you and you answer to me. It is better if no one knows I am involved, at least at the outset. Okay?"

"I get the picture. It sounds as if you know what you are doing," James said with obvious pleasure.

Lev was surprised and thankful at the outcome of this unexpected encounter. "Shalom, James! I think Christ was in this place today."

"Shalom," James replied. "I think he was also. Pray for me, Lev. I must not fail the Lord."

As James left, Lev felt an answer to his prayers had been sent. He wanted to get a counter-movement ready, but if he did, everyone would soon know that Lev was recruiting a resistance party. This would destroy the surprise in his actions.

He did not know what August's next move would be, but Lev noticed he was getting bolder. Satan wanted a foot in the new government, and he was pushing aggressively for it. Lev was determined to let him go unchallenged while he was outlining government functions. Since Satan really did not know how the government functioned so efficiently, his attempts to outline a workable plan were very vague. But no matter how democratic it sounded, once Satan got into office *he* would be the dictator.

It was important that Lev stay out of the issues until August and his committee started getting serious about intruding into office. Lev knew the Ancients would not renounce any of the advances being considered to take over the government. Their power and prestige was so great that they could crush and discredit August and his committee in a heartbeat. They knew that a real test was being put upon the people.

James Goes to Work

Lev didn't know what kind of support James could provide. He was nervous because he liked to pick the people he worked with, but leaving this to James would keep his name out of sight.

James proved to be heaven-sent. He turned out to be a quiet recruiter who used his connections in many countries to find responsible people who shared their vision. Every time Lev called him, he had added a name or two to their little movement, and his enthusiasm did not diminish. He was discreet and knowledgeable, knowing how to get information and make use of it. Most of all, he had become convinced that August and his committee served as a front for Satan. He inspired his people with a vision and wanted them committed to stand up and be counted when the time was ripe.

James was also showing his wisdom. He checked on Lev and the whole Aron family. He made sure he was not following another maverick with a private agenda. He was impressed with Lev's long service for the King and, more importantly, that he never failed at any undertaking. All who worked with him admired him, and no one found fault with his integrity. This was true of the whole Aron family and also of the Obadiahs. James became absolutely convinced that Lev was going to take the field against August and his committee.

Meanwhile, August was gaining confidence because there was no visible opposition. He was certain that Lev was a lame opponent who seemed incapable of any strong response. While there were people that were reticent to accept August's views, they were not antagonistic, so he felt his place in government was well underway. He was running his campaign unopposed. That was a tremendous comfort to him.

Several months passed while August and his committee kept up their campaign. He was being accepted as a candidate for office and there seemed to be no other contenders. Those who wanted to wait until the Ancients left office would not consider allowing their names to stand as possible candidates. Most people loved the Ancients and would do nothing that would indicate disrespect for them. But August and his committee were becoming bolder in their hints that the Ancients should begin sharing the seat of government with others.

Little Army Growing

Lev's little army was growing daily in numbers and in knowledge. They did not know who their leader was, but they knew everything August was doing and they did not like what they were seeing. They remained silent, however, giving no public opposition.

Week by week August was allowed to believe his way was clear, even though he occasionally checked on Lev to see if he was doing anything to thwart his moves. He could find nothing. Fortune was smiling upon him, and his confidence grew.

As long as no further moves were made toward taking over the government, Lev decided to let August continue uncontested. They were smooth operators, soft-spoken, full of concerns about the well-being of the citizens. Never was there a hint of personal ambition or ostentation on their part. They presented their case with all innocence. The increasing restlessness with the Ancients' lack of involving common people in their office was the only thing that belied their motive. It became increasingly obvious to Lev and his band of followers that August was planning to be a front-runner for office.

Lev knew that when somebody desires an office too much, they really disqualify themselves from holding that office. Personal desires indicate hidden ambitions that should not be gratified. In yesterday's world, it was a common practice among politicians who were not too concerned about either hidden or overt ambitions to grab for positions. The situation was much different now. The King would surely destroy anyone with personal ambitions. The world had six thousand years of that kind of leadership, and Christ was not going to allow another opportunity to surface.

August began to think, "Maybe the King is too kind to ask them to leave. Perhaps they need a little gentle persuasion."

August felt that since the King had done nothing to discourage his advances toward office, it was a good omen. Maybe Christ was secretly grateful for his agitation. August and his companions could have easily been discredited, but for some reason the King had allowed him to prosper. Perhaps this indicated he should push a little harder. Even the Ancients hadn't curtailed his activities. Could the King be restraining them? Maybe it was time to increase the pressure? He could always step back if the moves he made seemed too extreme. Few seemed to fault him. While August knew that Lev was opposed to him and his movement, he seemed ineffective.

Meanwhile Lev was working closely with James. He had over one hundred people pledged to the cause. They were fully informed on the Committee's moves from day one. They could all see the pattern of uninhibited ambition clearly at work. Though they were restless, James kept them restrained from making any personal moves.

Uncertainty Prevailed

Most people thought the Ancients would leave their offices when the thousand years ended, so discussion continued about that. Some thought that Christ was retaining them for some special reason; whereas, others could not understand the delay. Government had not previously been anyone's concern. The Ancients were appreciated, especially when people remembered how badly human governments had operated in the past. There were scandals, abuses of power, bribes, incompetence, insensitivities to the people's needs, greed, power, lust, decadence, and the list could go on and on. The Ancients, on the other hand, had served for the common good of all, tirelessly and wisely.

If the Ancients stayed in power forever, it would please most people. The only ones who might not like it would be those who wished to hold office themselves. This unfortunately was the position of August and his band of discontents. These were ideal candidates for Satan's enchantments and apparently they had not been overlooked by him. Confrontation was inevitable.

As the months rolled on, the Ancients were still in Jerusalem.

*"Satan shall be loosed out of his prison,
and shall go out to deceive the nations"
(Revelation 20:7, 8).*

Chapter Fifteen

Over a year had passed since August Hambers had formed
the Committee, which had first started to praise the Ancients
with just a gentle hint about their tenure of office being expired.
Repeated attempts to have them begin some transition of power
to the general population went by unheeded. The Ancients
remained silent. This only increased the agitation of those
waiting to take over the government. No one was ever asked
to assist with government despite their constant hints that they
would gladly participate on any level of operation if only asked.
Citizens for Self-Rule, or CSR, became a formal organization
led by August Hambers and the time had come for them to push
a little harder.

The CSR decided to organize campaigns to make the world
know their frustration with the silent treatment they had received
from the Ancients. They planned a massive rally with thousands
of demonstrators in Jerusalem. They did not ask permission this
time, but felt justified because of the amount of time that had
passed without receiving any response to their platform. The
Ancients had given no explanation other than they did not have
permission to leave office. It may have been a very good reason,
but it did not please the CSR.

Lev learned of this rally from James, who had heard of the
great planeloads of people coming into Jerusalem from all over
the world. Many were flying in on private planes filled with
people. It was time to call in his small band of recruits to come to

Jerusalem to stand in opposition. Lev knew that his forces would be outnumbered a hundred to one, but he had a close relationship with the man in charge of the television cameras. His name was Lee Fairfielding. Lev knew Lee was fully in sympathy with the Ancients staying in office forever, if needed.

Lev enlisted Lee's assistance, explaining that his people would be greatly outnumbered and wondered if he might arrange to place his small force in predetermined positions to be in full view of the cameras. Lee was more than happy to comply, so he told Lev the five sites where his cameras would be set up. He would not move the cameras, so Lev's opposition group would be in full view during the whole protest.

August and his thousands of protesters arrived on August 17, full of placards and enthusiastic people eager to spread their message. Their signs read: IS IT TIME FOR CHANGE? — SHOULDN'T YOU PREPARE REPLACEMENTS? — WE WILL MISS YOU, ANCIENTS — WHEN YOU ARE GONE WILL BE TOO LATE — GIVE US A CHANCE TO HELP — WE WILL STILL LOVE YOU WHEN YOU EXIT OFFICE — NO ONE IS IRREPLACEABLE — THE THOUSAND YEARS ARE ENDED — HOW ABOUT HELPING US IN TRANSITION?

They arrived full of zeal for their cause and spread over the city, not knowing where the cameras would be posted. They were everywhere and loud in their protests. However, they found Lev's little bands in five locations. To their dismay the cameras were set up right in front of Lev's recruits and their signs could be read clearly by all.

The Loyal Opposition

The signs of the loyal opposition read: STAY FOREVER ANCIENTS, YOU SERVED US WELL — SERVE US STILL, GO HOME CITIZENS FOR SELF-RULE — CHRIST'S CHOSEN ONES PLEASE STAY — RULE US FOREVER,

YIELD NOT TO SATAN — YOU MUST NOT LEAVE OFFICE, ANCIENTS — YOU ARE CHRIST'S APPOINTED RULERS — WE NEED YOU — CHRIST HAS NOT RELEASED YOU — DON'T LEAVE US NOW, SATAN WANTS YOU OUT.

August was furious to find he had been outmaneuvered. He accused Lee Fairfielding of unfair coverage of the news. He demanded to know how Lev had access to information as to where the cameras would be located.

Lee responded, "He asked me and I told him. It's that simple."

"Why weren't we given that information?" August demanded.

"You didn't ask. We never volunteer that information, but we never refuse it to those who ask. The same information would have been provided to your group, had you inquired," replied Lee indignantly.

"You realize you are distorting the news this day. All of Lev's posters are highly visible on TV screens, and ours are in the background and are often illegible. You cannot let this go on. I insist that you move your cameras to focus on my people. This is an embarrassment to my good people who are trying to serve the highest interests of the world by pressing for legitimate self rule," August demanded.

"I don't have a sufficient staff to make the changes you demand. Even if I did, I would not change the position of my cameras. I do not take orders from the public," Lee asserted.

August was angry. He realized that Lee was under no obligation to him, yet the impression left by the cameras showed all of the loyal opposition in the forefront. Their signs were favoring the Ancients remaining in power and this drove August wild.

He had to do something. The people living in Jerusalem were fiercely loyal to the Ancients. They had blocked the streets with vehicles and aircraft making it difficult for August to maneuver his people around. He found his only means of communication with his followers was by telephone because he was hemmed in. He didn't dare resort to violence, but he sorely wished he could. He finally was able to reach Lev in the midst of his distress.

August was frantic. Upon seeing Lev, he shouted, "Traitor. You have turned the sacrifices of my followers into a lame exercise. I thought you were of nobler mind than to indict my followers as servants of Satan. How could you even suggest that?" he demanded.

"Because Satan is loose and I think you are being duped by him," answered Lev more calmly than he felt.

"Oh, that is totally outrageous," cried August.

"The assault upon the Ancients was shameful," Lev answered firmly.

"Your insinuations are shocking," shouted August. "We stand for the highest principles. We want to insure an uninterrupted government once the Ancients leave office. What is the matter with that? Don't you love your fellow members of mankind enough to share our concerns?"

"You have created a problem where none exists. The Ancients will not leave behind a vacuum when their tenure of office ends. They will make all the provisions for continuance of government without having to resort to your help. Don't you understand that they remain in office at Christ's behest? Why are you trying to push them out?" Lev questioned him forcefully.

"Their rule was to end when the thousand years ended. They refuse to let anyone know what is going on inside the government. Why the secrecy? Do they have something to hide?" August demanded angrily.

"Why should they open their offices to anyone? They never did before the thousand years ended—why should they do it now? They still answer to the highest authority—why should they answer to you?" Lev retorted.

"You insist on describing us as Satan worshippers being led with rings in our noses, while you parade about as a knight in shining armor defending the government from being touched by unclean hands. You are a hypocrite posing as the defender of the elite and powerful. They do not need your signs and innuendos to protect their lofty thrones of power. Why don't you stand out of the way and let us poor mortals take our case to the people of the world?" raged August while some of his followers showed their disgust with Lev and his loyal opposition.

August forgot he was being recorded on television and his anger was being broadcast abroad. By the time he realized his mistake, it was too late. His bold and overbearing statements heartened his loyal followers, although some of them lost their ardor when they realized the possibility that Satan was deceiving them. They demanded some assurances from August that this was not true. He simply scoffed at the suggestion, claiming that his movement represented the people and their concern for good government. Would Satan be interested in something so pure?

The answer did not satisfy many of them, and they began deserting his cause. Realizing that he had lost the day, August decided to call off his crusade. He had really intended, Lev learned from some of his disillusioned followers, to use loudspeakers in front of the offices of the Ancients, challenging them to open their doors to the people. Instead, he was forced to call off his siege against the Ancients. Before admitting defeat that day, he quietly said to Lev, "You are one clever opponent. Next time I will not be taken by surprise. I must admit with your handful of followers you stole the show today. It is unfortunate that those who want continuance of good government were so badly treated."

Committed Opposition

"I know you will be back here, more subtle, more refined, but no matter how carefully you cloak your motives, August, you are still leading Satan's assault against the Ancients. I have no mandate to resist you. Naked principle causes me to resist. I cannot prevent your further efforts to steal control of the government, but I promise to remain in opposition. You have never answered questions about the fundamental need for your organization. You simply assume the Ancients will exit suddenly with only chaos left behind them. That is a terrible assumption and, needless to say, an incorrect one. Order is heaven's first law, and we have no reason to believe it will cease the day the Ancients leave office," Lev asserted.

"I cannot reason with you, Lev. Once you have judged our efforts as baneful, you persisted in your attacks. I will be better prepared next time. I am not a quitter either, Lev. I do not really think the Ancients have engaged you to attack me. If I did, I might have reason to weigh what you are saying, but you are just attacking our innocent endeavors to insure good government for reasons I cannot begin to understand," August said in parting.

"Shalom, August. Unfortunately you think only you are in control of your Citizens for Self-Rule. You are a convenient starting place for Satan to begin his work of deception. You cannot control the steamroller with which he is preparing to clear the office of the Ancients. I do not think you realize the fixation he has on getting control of the government. What was always his method? He offered Jesus 'all the kingdoms of the world and their glory' (Matthew 4:8-10). Obviously, he had them to give Jesus if he would yield to his suggestions. He is just using you as a pawn to get to the place he wants to go."

"How ridiculous! Lev, do you think I would knowingly lead Satan's advances? I understand that Satan is going to be destroyed. Would I lead people to their destruction? I do not want to be destroyed, nor would I lead others in that direction," snapped August.

"Have you ever heard of people being deceived?" asked Lev.

"Yes, of course, but do I look like some simpleton? You misjudge me, Lev. I know exactly what I am doing."

"I am glad you are so confident, August. All I know is that Satan is busy deceiving people, and I am sorry to say it, but I fear you *are* being deceived. I urge you to quit your tirade against the Ancients. They are not leaving until Christ releases them, so all your efforts to get them out of office will fail. You are not serving Christ, but Satan," Lev said very sincerely looking August in the eyes.

Many of his followers who were standing around listening to the exchange seemed to respond to Lev's remarks. One said, "Maybe he's right, August. We might be in danger of being destroyed as rebels against Christ. I am quitting. What's the hurry about getting the Ancients out of office, anyway?"

"Oh, don't you be deceived by this sweet talker," August responded.

Another said, "Maybe you are the sweet talker, August. You will have us destroyed if we continue our protests against the Ancients."

Many became seriously concerned that they were being mislead, and soon August was facing a number of his followers who were threatening to quit.

The Fearful and Uncertain Invited to Leave

August remained unmovable as he again affirmed the rightness of his cause. He said, "Those not fully persuaded should separate from our ranks. We don't need halfhearted believers in our cause. If you're fearful and uncertain, we don't want you. I would rather have a hundred people who are true believers on my side than a thousand doubters. Any who are not convinced in the rightness of our cause—leave!" August commanded.

To his surprise, many of his followers decided to leave and told him so. Lev stood by and watched the ranks of August's followers thin out.

August, red faced with fury, turned to Lev. "Are you satisfied now, Lev? You've had the victory today, but I am not a quitter and those with me are more solid than ever. You may have helped my cause by ridding me of the weak ones, 'thank you.' But I will be back, and you can count on it. I knew things were going along too easily. You are very clever, Lev. I'll concede that. Next time I will be better prepared."

Lev did not doubt August's resolve. He was committed to this deception and it would only be a matter of time until he would think of some other scheme to advance his Citizens for Self-Rule. However, Lev's followers stood firmly with him even more determined than ever as to the rightness of their cause. August lost a lot of ground that day. More people were frightened by his antics to set up self-rule before the Ancients left office. The people were not ignorant of the Scriptures that described Satan's activities after being released from the abyss, and they were very concerned lest they be found among the rebels.

Due to the great setback, August and his followers would need many months to collect new followers as well as to think of a new approach to further their cause. Life was so enjoyable now that few were willing to jeopardize it for an uncertain cause.

Lev found himself surrounded with many people who wanted to stand with the Ancients. He was not looking for great numbers of people, only for those who were genuinely convinced that the Ancients should stay in office until released of their duties by Christ. He could not interview those who volunteered that day, but he did take their names and phone numbers and turned them over to James, who had selected the competent support group that Lev used. The numbers Lev could count on were going to be enormously increased.

Lev was weary as he joined the throngs heading for their various homes. He was pleased with his loyal opposition forces and had left a good impression on the general public. Lev knew the devil had not finished his work of deception. The testing would become more severe.

"Cleanse thou me from secret faults"
(Psalm 19:12).

Chapter Sixteen

Lev couldn't stop thinking about the protest. Two particular conversations he had with members of August's crowd continued to haunt him, and he felt a desire to contact each of them

He remembered Eli Moshie, a very handsome man with great reserve and a charming personality. During all the turmoil of the day, Eli had pressed near Lev to ask, "Do you think this rally is a good idea?"

"I wouldn't be trying to offset it if it was," Lev responded.

"I thought it was at the outset, but the way it's going gives me pause," Eli had said with a perplexed frown.

"Give me your name, and we will talk later," Lev requested.

"Thank you," he said as he gave his name and phone number.

Lev phoned Eli the following evening.

"Shalom, Eli speaking, how may I help you," was his gentle reply.

"Shalom, this is Lev Aron, calling you as I promised."

"Oh, thank you for calling, Lev. I thought you might be too busy to remember me. You know, I am sorry I was ever in that rally."

"Where do you live?" Lev asked.

"By the Mediterranean Sea, not far from Haifa," he replied.

"Rather than just talk by phone, let me fly over to your place, and we can spend the supper hour and evening together," Lev suggested.

"That would be wonderful! I'll be waiting for you. I spent a troubled night, and want to remove myself from August's movement entirely. I did not belong with that crowd."

It was a beautiful flight, and Lev enjoyed the scenery by flying as low as was permitted. The countryside was lush with no barren places. As he neared the sea, the sunset was glowing with red golden-laced clouds in the western sky. Sails bobbing on the sea reflected its bright colors as Lev set his craft down on Eli's pad.

With the Rebels but Not a Rebel

Eli came running out to greet him. Lev hardly turned off the power and opened the door, when Eli was warmly shaking his hand and inviting him in. He said, "I am so glad you came, Lev. I really don't deserve your kindness after participating in that rally."

"All is not lost, Eli. I don't think you stepped over the line. If I thought you had, I wouldn't be here," Lev assured him.

Comforted, Eli smiled. "Come and refresh yourself, and we'll have supper."

Lev entered his lovely home where Eli had set the table on his terrace, overlooking the Mediterranean's brilliant sunset. After Eli asked Lev to seek the blessing on the food, they began to enjoy the Lord's bounty together. Lev asked Eli to tell his life's story, which he was eager to do.

"I was born in 1840 and lived at a good time in history. I was born in Europe but migrated to the United States as a boy. We lived in New York, and my father opened a little business selling clothing. He made a fair living, and I was able to get a good education for that time. I went to a private Jewish school where, along with my regular schooling, I learned to speak and read Hebrew. I was to finish my college education and could hardly wait until I would be married to a girl from my home village to whom I was betrothed. However, her letters to me became less frequent and finally they stopped. I learned that a rather rich Jewish young man had apparently succeeded in winning her hand in marriage. I was devastated."

Lev sat quietly listening as Eli continued sharing his experiences, while the evening sky deepened into the richest palette of colors.

Lost Love Can Live Again in Sweeter Relationships

"I have learned in my present life that there is no reason that I cannot share my life with Natalie and with every other loving person. I have been bonded to so many more people since the regeneration than ever in my original life. Instead of recreating the past, I can create a new and living relationship more beautiful than the past could ever be."

"Yes, Eli, you are correct. We have to learn to love on a higher plane—the way God and Christ love," Lev observed.

"Getting back to yesterday's activities, Lev, I want you to know if you need help in any future confrontation with the Citizens for Self-Rule, I will be glad to volunteer. I feel as though I was misled and want to make it right now. I will do anything I can to help others see the truth. I do not want to rebel against the Ancients or Christ's future plans. I trust them completely and know they will provide what is best for us."

"Thank you, Eli. I appreciate your confession and I will call on you if I need you! Thank you for the supper, and now I'd better be going. Do not forget to stand for righteousness on every occasion," Lev exhorted. The men hugged each other and Lev left for home, grateful he had the opportunity to guide another heart to the Lord's ways.

The next day, his thoughts turned to the other person he had talked to back at the protest. She had waited until August left and the crowds thinned, when with a weak voice she approached him saying, "Mr. Aron, I am very troubled by the events of this day. I want to talk to you when it is convenient. My name is Fiona Kierly. I hope the good Lord will forgive me."

"Just give me your phone number, Fiona, and I will call you soon. What time of the day or evening is convenient for you?" Lev asked.

"Well, afternoons and evenings I am generally home and would be free to talk. I promise not to take too much of your time," she added as she gave Lev her number and address on a card.

"Don't worry about my time. I plan to be around forever, so what is a little time spent with a friend?" Lev assured her with a laugh.

"I appreciate your willingness to talk with someone who apparently has lost her good sense," she said sadly.

"Shalom, Fiona, I promise you will hear from me."

Lev called her that evening. She lived in Scotland and the time of his call would be early evening in her time zone.

A voice answered, "Shalom, this is Fiona Kierly."

"Shalom, Fiona. This is Lev Aron calling as you requested. I hope this is a convenient time."

"Oh, thank you, Mr. Aron, I was hoping you wouldn't forget me."

A Cry for Help

"No, it's not like in the old days. Besides, I could not forget you. I thought I heard a little cry for help in your voice — was I right?"

"Aye, you judge correctly, Mr. Aron. I was very distressed at the close of that day and still I am distressed. Let me tell you my story, so you will know how I happened to be in that group of Citizens for Self-Rule."

"Please do. I love to learn about people," Lev said encouragingly.

"I will try to make it short. In my former life, I was born a healthy and happy girl to wonderful parents. Everything was fine until I developed curvature of the spine. In those days there was no remedy, and gradually I became more and more bent and twisted. I had the nicest boyfriend, but at last he began to think I was grotesque. I grew into adulthood a deformed woman and all hopes for a normal life ended. My parents cared for me with great kindness, but they, too, were heartbroken as they watched my once lovely body became deformed. I became rather helpless, and my parents had to devote their lives to my care.

"As my parents became older, they could not care for me any longer; it was too hard to lift me. Finally a younger aunt took me into her home. However, she was not equal to the task of caring for me either, and she would often express her anger and frustration with me. I was so unhappy I decided to swallow a bottle of sleeping pills. I took them in the morning as soon as she left, knowing that when she would return she would find my lifeless body. Then she would be free of the burden of caring for me."

The Rejected Ugly and Deformed

"You can imagine my joy when I came back to life, straight and beautiful—a complete human being. I stared in the mirror for the longest time. I could have danced for joy, but I thought that this was a dream or hallucination and that I would awaken with my old deformed body at any moment," Fiona confessed.

"That must have been a thrilling experience, Fiona, to find God had given you a body that pleased Him. All your dreams of being made whole again were realized in a moment. And I can imagine the joy of your parents when they returned to life to find a beautiful daughter standing before them. God has made up to each individual for his or her former lack. Those who suffered from disabilities really appreciated being healed and made whole. The deaf sang for they could finally hear, the blind saw light and beauty, the lame leaped as a hart (Isaiah 35:5,6)," Lev reminded Fiona.

"I knew you were right when I realized the crowd I was with did not appreciate the better judgment of the Ancients properly. Their decisions, whatever they may be, deserve the utmost respect at all times. I never want to side with that crowd again under any circumstances," Fiona affirmed.

"You must not rebel against the Ancients either, because one of these times 'fire' *is* going to come down out of heaven and consume those who do," Lev reminded her.

"I tremble when I think of how close I came to rebellion. Here I am an intelligent person who knows exactly what the Bible teaches on this subject. I thought the praise first shown toward the Ancients was exemplary, but now I'm not sure how genuine it was. August and that whole movement seem to be pushing the Ancients, and I don't like that," confessed Fiona.

"The Bible has many stories about those who rejected the leaders God had provided them. The Ancients have served humanity in a way that no others could have, and they deserve our full support and admiration. Under Christ's reign they worked day and night to remedy the world's problems. They dealt with individuals who were punished and needed healing. I was one of them who had my arm paralyzed, but there were billions like me who also resorted to violence and had to be punished and healed. They operated twenty-four hours a day so no one had to wait to receive their personal attention," Lev reminded Fiona.

"I do not need to be reminded of their love and faithfulness," Fiona explained. "I spoke to Sarah to tell her arrangements had been made for my mother to come back. She told me the day and hour of her return and then said, 'She will be so happy to see you whole and beautiful, I wish I could be there to share the happiness of that reunion.' It was so. My mother just burst into tears of joy when she saw me. She thought I was an apparition. Then she clung to me, feeling me to be sure I was real. She asked, 'How did you get healed?' My explanation seemed like a fairy tale to her," Fiona reminisced. "The same was true when my father returned to life. He kept saying, 'Fiona, my little girl, you are so beautiful, let me hold you in my arms so you don't disappear from me.'"

"Every resurrection story I hear is just marvelous," Lev effervesced. "I never get tired of hearing them."

"Well, one thing is for certain! I am not going with August or any other group that even hints at what the Ancients should do," she said.

"Thank you, Fiona. I don't know if we will have another confrontation, but if we do, I will call you. Meanwhile, stand up for the Ancients, as they deserve your utmost respect and devotion. Encourage everyone you have contact with to do the same. You know Satan is trying to seduce as many as he can to disobey, and the danger is very real," Lev exhorted.

"Thank you for calling, Mr. Aron."

"I am going to let you go now. If you ever have any questions you think I can help you with, you have my number. I will keep your name on the list of those loyal to the King and his Worthies," Lev said. "Shalom."

Seeking an Invitation

He'd barely hung up with Fiona when the phone rang. Lev answered, "Shalom."

"Shalom. I have been wondering how you are doing. You haven't told me about your trip to Jerusalem," Rebekah chided.

"I'm sorry, Rebekah. If you invite me over for a cup of tea, I will share two delightful stories with you," Lev said with a laugh.

"I guess I can spare a cup of tea," Rebekah said in good humor.

"It has been a full day and I am tired. How about tomorrow night, Rebekah?" questioned Lev.

"Okay, it's a date," she chuckled.

"And after that he must be loosed a little season"
(Revelation 20:3).

Chapter Seventeen

August's party of Citizens for Self-Rule remained silent for almost a year. The rally had seriously damaged his credibility. Everybody knew that "fire" would come and destroy rebels, and no one was anxious to be destroyed.

One morning Lev's phone rang loudly waking him from sound sleep. It was 2:00 a.m. What was going on? Lev managed to rouse himself and pick up the phone. As he cleared his throat to speak, a voice interrupted him, "Shalom. This is Moses. I am sorry to call you at this hour, but I need to advise you not to interfere in any way with the forthcoming protests. Thank you." Then there was silence.

Lev now sat on the edge of his bed fully awake. He realized he had not said a word. Moses must have used an untraceable phone. Lev realized that something of great importance was about to happen. First, Moses had secretly asked him to provide a loyal opposition to August Hambers and the Citizens for Self-Rule. Now he was being told not to do anything. Obviously, the time was at hand for another orchestrated move to take place against the Ancients. Lev had heard nothing of it. He felt a great sense of apprehension. What was going to happen?

He decided not to tell anyone about this message. If Moses had wanted others to know, he would not have used such extraordinary means not to be heard. He knew Lev would be alone at that hour, so no one else would even know if Lev had received a phone call, much less what it was about.

He called the airports in Israel to find out if there was unusual activity. Sure enough, the following week flights into Israel were booked solid. He was stunned by the realization that surely this was going to be the final protest by those who were determined to have their demands met.

Being silent and inactive was against everything Lev had always been about, and his adrenaline was pumping. He could not sleep anymore that night, but waited until first rays of light to shave and shower. Before even eating breakfast, he went to his computer to check all the flight bookings. He was astonished. This gathering would dwarf all previous assemblies.

As Lev went through his daily activities all that week, the protest was never far from his mind. On the day before it was scheduled, he decided to go to the airport to get a firsthand sense of things. Hordes of people were everywhere. It was impossible to even estimate the numbers. Just as he was about to leave, he saw Tom Tilean, a refined and articulate man on August Hambers' team, disembarking. Tom also saw him. Not wishing to give away his knowledge, Lev offered a friendly smile and said, "You've chosen the best time to visit the Holy Land. It is beautiful right now with all the flowers still blooming and the heat of summer past."

"Thank you, Lev. You are very gracious to welcome me to your beloved land. You are blessed to live here. The Lord saved this land for Father Abraham and his descendants, so it must be special," Thomas remarked.

Lev was glad that Tom did not inquire what he was doing there. It just looked like an accidental meeting, which indeed it was.

Lev quickly left for his aircraft, not wanting to be noticed by anyone else. Now he was certain what was happening. If Tom Tilean were here, August Hambers would soon be also, if not already. This was going to be the final gathering of the voices seeking change. While flying home, Lev noticed an unusual number of private planes flying toward the capital. The numbers assembling in Jerusalem must be very great indeed. Of course, it was the time of the Feast of Tabernacles and that may have been the time chosen to cover the real reason for this assembly. The Feast of Tabernacles or Feast of Booths was kept in the fall of the year for seven days (Leviticus 23:39-43), as a Thanksgiving celebration for the harvesting of crops.

When he arrived home, Lev quickly called his assistant, James, to tell him what was happening. James was leaving for his work.

As always, James was ready to serve at a moment's notice. "What do you want me to do, Lev? Shall I call my team to meet us in Jerusalem?"

He was stunned when Lev said, "No."

The sheer magnitude of those assembling at Jerusalem seemed to be a logistics problem. How would Jerusalem feed all these people? Such disproportioned numbers would exhaust the food supply of the region. However, no one needed to worry. The problem had been anticipated, and each attendee had brought sufficient dried fruit of "paradise" with him or her so that by only adding water they would be well fed.

The assembled crowds were courteous and law-abiding. They had brought little tents and set them up along the roads and green areas in the city. The residents opened their homes so that those needing restroom facilities and showers could use them. There also were hundreds of homes that had been left by the 'goats,' and these were being used as small inns. The residents of the city placed all fruit that they didn't need in bowls in front of their houses for anyone to help themselves.

The reason for this massive gathering was not immediately clear. The Feast of Tabernacles was only kept in token form, so it was a surprise to find such a crowd gathering. There had been no announcement of any protest meeting or anything of that sort. The sheer number of those gathered indicated something very big was about to happen. None of the leaders had as yet stepped forward so there was an air of mystery about the gathering. It all looked so innocent that it was impossible to imagine what the results would be. No one was carrying signs, and no one was acting unruly.

A Determined Crowd

Still the crowd had gathered for some purpose and was not about to leave until the Ancients gave answers. Planes were still unloading thousands of people each day. One would think that the Ancients would have limited the number of people that could come, but they said nothing as the people poured in from all over the world. They only asked that the citizens of the city to be as hospitable as possible, and to try to accommodate as many as they could.

The First Day of the Feast of Tabernacles

At last, on the first day of the feast Tom Tilean and August Hambers stepped forward to address the masses. They were cheered loudly. They had set up closed circuit cameras so the entire throng could hear their words. Public television was carrying the whole event before the world, for not since the Battle of Armageddon had so many assembled here.

"In the spirit of the Feast of Tabernacles, we will share a feast of thanksgiving," Tom Tilean began. "We no longer gather our fruit that we depend on for life at this time of year, but every day is a feast of harvesting the trees of life. We still harvest some food such as grapes at this season, but it has become symbolic for the final harvest of the year and, as always, is abundant with God's blessings. How thankful we are! We will start our thankful week with hymns of praise and prayer."

After two hymns and an opening prayer, Tom Tilean introduced August Hambers. "My friends, I give you your faithful leader for Citizens for Self-Rule—August Hambers."

August strode up to the microphone and in his resonant voice began his flowery oration. "Dear fellow citizens, it is with thankful heart that I express my gratitude to those faithful servants of the Lord, the Ancient Worthies, who day and night have busied themselves tending to our needs. While we could not see them in action, we were very much aware that they were doing something right, for our government has been flawlessly tending to our needs. Nothing was overlooked. Never were they too busy to tend to a private call or to civic need.

"We only have words of praise for their long and tireless service. Of criticism—there is none. We want to thank them sincerely from the bottom of our hearts. We can only say to them, 'Well done thou good and faithful servants.' It is with sad hearts that we have come to realize that their tenure in office is soon to end and that they may experience a change of nature and be taken from us to heaven. Oh, yes, we are told of these faithful men and women, 'Of whom the world was not worthy' (Hebrews 11:38). So surely God has something better in store for them. When that time comes for them to leave the good earth, we desire to have a seamless government in place so that the same good services will continue unabated. We know we will never exceed their unerring capabilities or even come close to equaling them, but we are bound to the same principles of righteousness and truth— and that will not change, I assure you.

"We also want to assure you, dear friends and citizens, and the Ancients alike, that we are not here to run them out of office or to wrest from them what Christ has given to them. Yet, we do ask them to consider the need for continuous government when they leave office. We want to learn from them, if possible, the inner workings of government so we can continue their intelligent management of all government functions.

"We hope our leaders will be entreated by us and consider our plea to be made aware of what our future duties may entail. We are going to wait for an answer from the Ancients until the eighth day. That should give them time to consult with Christ. We will not contest the answer, but will abide by their word, whatever it may be. That will show that we are serious in our desire to do all things as they would want them done. Therefore, we hope to meet with representatives of the Ancient Worthies on the eighth day and shall be expecting an answer. Thanks to the Ancients for considering our plea. Shalom, and may God bless you."

The Crowd Was Feeling Its Strength

There was abundant applause and the crowd began to feel its strength in numbers. Some began shouting—"August for Prime Minister" again and again. He waved his palms to calm their enthusiasm.

"Order is heaven's first law."

The crowd responded. August had laid out his plan, and they had to wait for an answer. But would they remain so docile should the answer not be to their liking? Mob psychology was responsible for great evils—the greatest was the death of our Lord Jesus. It was clearly Satan's way of getting things done throughout history. As people multiplied in the earth, he had often used this method to work his mischief.

Beautiful new music had been composed for this event and was played over loudspeakers. This was followed by hymns of thanksgiving that were appropriate to the Feast of Tabernacles. The music tranquilized the people who were assembled, keeping them calm and in a pleasant mood. Even the citizens of the area enjoyed and joined in the singing.

August Hambers was very curious as to why Lev had not led a countermovement. He knew Lev was not the type to quit a battle, though his absence certainly made for a smoother event. Perhaps he was coming around to their way of thinking although, knowing Lev, August doubted that. Why did he decide not to be in opposition all of a sudden?

During the lunch break, August decided to call Lev and tell him he was missed at today's festivities. He was not expecting him to be home, but was pleasantly surprised to hear his voice. "Shalom, this is Lev speaking."

"Shalom, this is your old friend, August Hambers. Why aren't you here in Jerusalem, Lev?"

"I guess I didn't want to put a damper on your celebration. I thought I might come on the seventh day. I promise not to upstage you in any way. You don't mind if I dialogue with your troops, do you?" Lev asked intently.

"If I said 'Yes, I mind,' would you come anyway?" August said ruefully.

"I'm afraid I might. I have been known to be contrary at times," Lev responded.

"Why would you leave your home when you can see everything in the comfort of your living room on television? Wouldn't that be better?" August asked.

"That may be true, but I like to discuss issues with people, especially if an opposing view needs to be aired. You surely sanction free speech, don't you?" Lev questioned and they ended their conversation.

Tom Tilean Speaks

That afternoon the festivities continued with inspiring music, all originally composed for the event. The atmosphere was more of a party than a protest. There were no placards or signs to indicate discontent of any kind. Everybody seemed on his or her best behavior. This certainly did not seem like a rally Satan would sponsor.

Tom Tilean was to give the address. He was such a gifted speaker that he could hold a crowd's rapt attention while reading from a dictionary. Afterwards, the orchestra again played strains of the hauntingly beautiful music that drifted in the afternoon breezes. It gave the whole presentation a very innocent and charming air. The entire day's proceedings were so conducted that only if one failed to analyze the whole procedure, he might be led into thinking it was honorable enough. Even Lev felt that they did a masterful job as he watched the events on television.

"And when the thousand years are expired,
Satan shall be loosed out of his prison,
and shall go out to deceive the nations
which are in the four quarters of the earth, Gog and Magog,
to gather them together to battle:
The number of whom [is] as the sand of the sea.
And they went up on the breadth of the earth,
and compassed the camp of the saints about, and the beloved city:
and fire came down from God out of heaven, and devoured them.
And the devil that deceived them was cast into the lake of fire"
(Revelation 20:7-10).

Chapter Eighteen

For the first few days of the Feast, the crowds seemed peaceful and happy and did nothing to arouse criticism from the local people. There were music, singing, and speeches every day. Other activities were games and performances, all harmonious with a spirit of thanksgiving and celebration.

Lev Appears the Seventh Day

On the seventh day of the Feast of Tabernacles celebration, Lev landed at a friend's house in the city of Jerusalem. The friend was out of town for work and had invited Lev to use his home. This was a blessing because landing space was at a premium in Jerusalem. It was only a short walk to the staging area and Lev arrived full of energy. He was alone and just quietly stopping to chat with different people as he wandered about.

Lev had collected fresh fruit from his trees and his neighbors generously supplied him with extra. He carried a big bag with him and handed it out as he went. He saved some for August and Tom, just in case they might enjoy some. He appeared at the staging area where he found the two leaders looking a little frayed. To his surprise they welcomed the fresh fruit and thanked him for being so thoughtful.

"Oh, I thought you might need some fresh fruit after a long week. Keeping everybody happy for a week must be difficult," Lev said with a smile.

Both men stood owl-faced. August replied, "Thank you, Lev, this is quite a treat. I must say you are full of surprises. First you don't form your usual opposition and now you're even feeding the enemy."

"I promise I won't be joining forces with you," Lev assured. "I think I'll run along and see how your troops are faring."

Lev planned to stay longer, but quickly changed his mind when he read the mood of the desperate crowd, and left as soon as possible.

The Eighth Day

The crowd did not have a restful night. August and Tom began to have a sense of foreboding as soon as Lev left them. Not only did they not rest well, but they found themselves dreading approaching the headquarters of the Ancient Worthies for the answers they had sought. It was obvious their requests wouldn't be granted, but they feared what the consequences would be. They were not ignorant of the Scriptures.

The morning air was chilled, with no sun to warm anyone's bones. The assembled crowd reflected the gloom. The mass of people pressed in forcing August and Tom up to the entrance of the offices of the Ancients. No one came out and no answer to their request was given. The crowd was already restless and frustrated, and waiting for an answer was making them more irritable. After a half hour had passed they began to chant, "Don't ignore us," over and over.

Still no one responded. August and Tom were no longer in control of the crowd which was now chanting, "When are you leaving office?" The clamor arose in intensity and anger. The crowds were in no mood for a negative answer. They were in open rebellion and anger was in their hearts.

Some of the crowd broke loose and were about to force open the doors of the offices.

Suddenly the door opened and out strode Moses, Abraham, David and Daniel. They stood in front of the defiant crowds, tall and stately. A nervous, fearful hush fell over everyone. Moses spoke calmly and with authority. "Let your leaders come forward."

August and Tom, white with anxiety, stepped up, trembling with fear. August said, "Our humble apologies for the conduct of the crowd. No one was authorized to seek entrance into your sanctuaries."

Moses said, "Our doors are always open to holy men and women seeking whatever assistance we can give them. But they are not open to rebellious, defiant people who are demanding what is not God's will for them."

"We Will Be Leaving Office in a Matter of Days"

"We will be leaving office and this earth in a matter of days. But we will not leave our positions to those who seek them. Holy men and women will serve in our place. Only the meek will be given any power, and then it will only be for a short while. The offices we leave will be filled every four years by people who do not seek them," answered David.

As if a balloon had been popped, the power-hungry were deflated. Poor August, his face was ashen.

The sheer numbers began squeezing tighter around the offices of the Ancients. "They encompassed the camp [temporary dwelling place] of the saints about" (Revelation 20:9).

Suddenly the sky grew very dark. The air became heavy and the hair on the people's heads began to prickle as though charged with electricity. It was almost like the day of Armageddon. Silence filled the streets as their situation became apparent.

Moses lifted up his hands to heaven as he spoke. "Ye rebels and followers of Satan must share in the judgment of God this day. You are being destroyed because of your sinful and rebellious hearts. You have reached the end of your treachery and rebellion." There was no microphone, but his voice was heard clearly and loudly throughout Jerusalem.

Fire Comes Down From God

A roar of fire was heard and instantly the rebellious people disappeared, along with Satan their leader. They evaporated and were gone. The sun began to shine brightly and the birds to sing as though no protest had ever crowded the city.

News of what happened flashed around the earth. Strangely there was no mourning; no funerals, no eulogies, no weeping and no heartfelt sorrow. The news that Satan had been consumed along with his sympathizers was a joy to the whole earth. The moment of his release from his prison had not been like this. Then it felt like a spirit of discontent was coming upon people from nowhere. Most people did not succumb, but the "seed of the serpent" (Genesis 3:15) could not resist his voice. They followed their father, the devil, into the second death.

After the "goats" were destroyed the people of earth had inherited what Adam had lost. The "sheep" that remained enjoyed untested perfection. That is why Satan was not destroyed, but only kept in the "abyss." Just as Adam and Eve were tested after being created, so everyone needed to demonstrate that they lived the commandment, "Love the Lord thy God with all thy heart, and with all thy soul, and with all thy mind.... Thou shalt love thy neighbor as thyself" (Matthew 22:37-39). Those that remained now had their names written in the "Lamb's book of life" (Revelation 21:27). They were worthy of everlasting life in a world without end.

"And there shall be no more curse:
but the throne of God and of the Lamb shall be in it;
and his servants shall serve him;
And they shall see his face;
and his name shall be in their foreheads.
And there shall be no night there;
and they need no candle, neither light of the sun;
for the Lord God giveth them light:
and they shall reign for ever and ever"
(Revelation 22:3-5).

Chapter Nineteen

The Ancients declared a cessation from all work or activity. On the day after the eighth day there was to be a truly festive holiday week for all mankind who had survived the deceptions of the devil. The meek people did inherit the earth as an everlasting possession. The trial and testing time was over and those that remained had proved their fidelity to God.

The Ancients announced they would be taken from earth to a heavenly reward because they had pleased God. What that entailed even they did not fully comprehend, but they knew that a heavenly reward would be even richer and sweeter than the perfected earth. They said they would select some people who had shown exceptional dedication and service to mankind, and who had no aspiration to hold office, to manage earth's affairs. For the remainder they would accept volunteers from each of the countries and then select them by lot. They also encouraged families to volunteer together, because God was a family God. Every nation would be represented in ratio of its total population.

Four years of service would be required and then they would be released. They would not be called again until everyone had occupied office for four years. When eternity is before mankind, time is looked at differently.

They would be instructed for one week by the Ancients and then be in charge of earth's affairs. Government was pure and simple in a perfect world. All decisions had to be made for the common good. No one served in government for personal advantage or aggrandizement. The age of politicians had ended forever.

Aron and Obadiah Families Sought

Early on the day the announcement was made concerning the departure of the Ancients, Moses gave Lev a call.

"Shalom, this is Moses. The Ancients wish to express their gratitude to you for following our wishes so completely during the recent crisis. We could have dealt with that situation very differently, but we knew Satan and his followers needed to be exposed, so we remained silent. We were thankful your early loyal opposition movement encouraged those who needed to hear of the truth of our situation. We could not leave until we were released and that has not happened until now.

"We, under the direct instruction of Christ, wish you to be the new Prime Minister of earth, Lev. Your office will be for four years. Of course, there is no special temporal gain to be had, there will be no emergencies and no impossible situations will arise. It only involves wise and thoughtful planning to insure that the resources of earth are used to best advantage.

"We are not offering you this privilege as payment of any kind for previous services rendered, but you have been chosen because you know how to work with people, and this quality will make your administration a happy one. You must always seek the common good, being careful not to harm anyone in the process.

"We are calling your parents, Ariel and Hannah, your brother, Jacob, and his former wife, Rachel, and their daughter, Annie; your former wife, Rebekah, and your son, Allon, plus Benjamin and Deborah Obadiah for positions in government. We have had many others who have served faithfully when called to help, and we are also contacting them. We will have the new staff pulled together and functioning properly before we leave."

"Well," Lev exclaimed, "I am overwhelmed with your confidence in me. I will serve our King to the best of my ability. I always said, 'I feel sorry for the people who replace the Ancients in government. At their best they will look pretty shabby.' Now I will have to experience my own prophecy." But his face was beaming all the while.

"When we began to govern, the world was in a pretty sorry state. Having heavenly hosts as our police force was imperative. We soon had the attention of the people, and that enabled us to bring order out of chaos. To his glory, Christ led us all the way. We had perfect love, wisdom, justice and power as the governing principles, and that insured success. Christ deserves all the credit—all we did was obey him. That is all you must do as well. Christ still has all authority in heaven and earth. Just follow his gentle leadings," advised Moses.

"I am sure that I will be given the grace to succeed. I always have been supplied with grace in every time of need. I want you to know that I never hoped for such a position, and it is rather humbling to admit to my poor qualifications. However, I will never say 'no' to our King," Lev assured.

"Good, Lev, arrange your affairs to be with us the day before your training in office. Your homes will become guest homes while you are living in Jerusalem. All the homes of those destroyed also will become guest homes. This will give us a lot of facilities that the human race is going to need because the time has come for everyone to enjoy the provisions God has prepared for everyone to be happy," Moses said.

"It is so kind of you to have families serving in the office together. That used to be the vice of tyrants and politicians to bring their relatives into posh positions, kind of 'winners take all.' But now it honors the families in the highest sense by having them hold office together," Lev observed.

God Is a Family God

"Yes, God is a family God. He created the family as the best environment for children and it is still good for all God's children. We are all so thrilled that we were able to serve during Christ's reign. And now! Now we shall see the face of God at last and also of our beloved Savior! Rejoice with us! Shalom, Lev."

No sooner had he hung up than the phone rang again.

"Shalom, Lev, it's Rebekah. I heard the good news and wanted to be the first to congratulate you, Prime Minister Lev."

"Thank you, Assistant Prime Minister. All kidding aside, how will we ever fill the offices of some of the greatest people this world has ever known? We are not worthy to tie their shoelaces, much less sit in their offices," Lev observed.

"One good thing is, Lev, we won't be separated as often as before. It is wonderful to have families working together. I hope the loving family arrangement will flow outward to those who have to deal with us. I will miss my little piece of paradise," Rebekah sighed.

"I was thrilled that they asked your father and mother to serve. The Obadiahs have helped to make a greenhouse of the world. Their work made paradise worldwide and was the single most significant factor in the physical healing of the world," Lev commented.

"That reminds me, I'd better call my folks or they will think their daughter is too busy to have time for them. I cannot think of anyone more respected than they are," Rebekah observed.

"I was planning on touring the world before Moses called. I guess that will have to wait. Anyway, call your folks and welcome them aboard the new government replacing the Ancients," Lev laughed. "Shalom, Rebekah."

The phone kept ringing with congratulations. The Ancients released the news shortly after they confirmed their plans with Lev and various family members. Everyone knew the Ancients would be leaving this world and that was sad news. The people thought that when the "little season" was over, the Ancients would spend some time out of office as guests of the various nations. The world wanted to get to know them personally and, in some way, show their gratitude to these towering leaders who led them faithfully into the Kingdom of God on earth.

During this week of rest and world holiday, many nations wanted to meet the Ancients, but they made it clear that no gifts should be given them for they were leaving earth and could take nothing with them. However, they could receive all the love and affection that everyone wished to give, and that they could take with them as treasures from earth to heaven.

Obadiahs and Arons spend the Last Holiday with the Ancients

The holiday week passed with the whole earth rejoicing. Those remaining knew that eternity was before them, and that God would be their God and they would be His children. Satan was destroyed never again to cast his baneful influence over mankind. Never was such deep joy and serenity felt than at this time. God had accepted the human race as his restored family, and they were accorded all the joys as the "sons of God." God's will was done on earth, even as done in heaven.

By the end of the week the Ancients could feel the love and affection of the people for them as never before. It reminded Moses of his last days on earth with Israel. He had led them forty years and endured all their stubborn and sinful ways. Yet, he loved the people and at the end of his life the people truly loved him. When they had finally settled down and were to enter the Promised Land, Moses was taken. How they longed to have him lead them into the Promised Land, but that was not to be, for God was taking Moses from them. God took Moses up to Mt. Nebo, to Pisgah's height, and let him see the Promised Land, but he was not to enter it. He was buried in a valley of Moab in an unmarked gravesite (Deuteronomy 34:5,6).

Again, God was taking Moses and all the Ancients up to a place with a full view of the Promised Land, not to be buried, but to be with Him. God had something better for such heroes of faith. The world had been given better leadership than they really deserved, and now they realized that God would not spare them to the earth any longer. They were God's treasures and He would take them to Himself. They also became treasures to those on earth. Now that they were to be taken, the people realized how great would be their loss.

The week was a love feast with an outpouring of appreciation for the tireless work of the Ancients. So much of their service had been taken for granted. Their wonderful skills of instruction were a phenomenon never before attained in the field of education.

By the time the last day of festivities came the earth was happy, but tears were seen in everyone's eyes.

When Lev and all his family members arrived in Jerusalem, the Ancients warmly received them. Other representatives from all over the world, who had contributed to the needs of the Ancients by filling emergency situations, had also arrived to get acquainted with one another and with the Ancients. They would have to wait until the morrow to learn about the work they were to do, but this day had been set aside for them as a final climax. Not only did they meet all the prominent Ancients, but also many who had worked without much visibility, yet were nevertheless precious in God's sight. Paul mentioned some of the Ancient

Worthies in his hall of fame, but he said they were too numerous to mention (Hebrews 11). It was grand to meet them all, even though time was too limited to learn of their faithful past from each of them firsthand. It was sufficient to know they had all pleased God.

Another surprise was in store for everyone. Adam and Eve would share in the first pick of earth's new cabinet. When Lev learned that Adam and Eve would be in government, he tried to give his position to them, but they did not have the experience in the technical world, so he learned the decision was not reversible. However, everyone was delighted to be working with the first human pair.

When asked about their heavenly assignment, Moses replied, "We have less knowledge than you do about the office that you will fill. Who knows what heaven is like? We know only that we will not need food or water or air to breathe. Neither will we need sleep. Our bodies must be changed to a spiritual state for we know that 'flesh and blood cannot inherit the Kingdom of God.' Yet we know the joy that will be ours in seeing our God and Christ as they are, face-to-face. We all love them while not having seen them, but it will certainly be better when we shall behold their glory. It is this thought that makes us tingle with excitement. So as much as we sorrow in leaving our human family behind, we look forward to our change with unspeakable joy. We will also meet all the members of the Christ body, all one hundred and forty-four thousand of them. So that will be a magnificent homecoming. What wondrous things has God reserved for those who love Him!"

Departing Sorrow

Sarah said, "We would have been happy to stay on earth. We love the earth and our wonderful family here. There has been an ineffable joy in working with mankind as, with painstaking efforts, they reached up to regain the image of God in their hearts."

Abraham said, "We were privileged to have God speak to us. Indescribable! God Almighty condescending to speak to us, and we knew it was the Almighty! We wrote of our experiences wondering who would believe our report. Yet countless thousands not only believed, but they dedicated their lives to the visions that we received. At times it looked like it was vain to serve God, but see now how faith in God has been rewarded."

John the Baptist spoke, "I beheld the Only Begotten of the Father, full of grace and truth. All of my brothers and sisters were not as privileged as I. They spoke of the Messiah who should come, but I was blessed in preparing the way of the Lord. Yet, I died a comparatively easy death, not knowing that our Lord would be crucified. The only sinless man in the whole world, and they crucified him. Satan was truly the god of that old world."

David said, "Yes, Jesus was my son, my offspring, but I also called him my Lord (Psalm 110:1). He was the one through whom God promised me that I would have a son to sit on the throne of the Lord forever. Now it will be my privilege to see my son in glory. Even though I am his grandfather of some sort, yet I will be bending low before his throne. The ways of the Lord are too deep for me; how can I know them?"

Huldah joined in saying, "Seeing this is a small testimony meeting on the part of the Ancients, I would like to add mine. We have been given opportunities of service that I never felt I deserved. I was one of the prophetesses the Lord used (II Kings 22:14), and that was because there were no men worthy to act as his prophets. I spoke the Word of the Lord and I believed with all my heart in that Word. I am surprised to be rewarded so richly. We have been keeping company with some of the best people of earth. That was enough reward for me. Then to our amazement we have been told that God has invited us up higher!"

The day was spent in listening to the Ancients as they looked forward to their change. There was a joy that could be felt and a oneness of spirit among them. They had given of their time and strength in an extravagant manner without the world really knowing and appreciating all that they did. They did not have to keep track of all the dead for that was done by Christ, who also raised the dead in their proper order and time, overlooking no one. Such flawless performance could only be true of those possessing the divine nature. Yet, the miracle of the regeneration was so great that looking back on the accomplishment of so much in such a limited time was almost staggering to contemplate.

The New Administration Takes Office

The following day Lev and all the new appointees to office were shown their respective offices and duties. The workload was such that it could be done in a workday easily without any pressure. There were no piles of paper anywhere. The Ancients had perfect recall, and when something was agreed upon it was done. The New Law Covenant was the Constitution of a perfect human race, so all that was required was the oversight of general needs.

The offices were very plain with no large desks or posh furniture. Lev found his office rather Spartan, but it suited him fine. His mother and dad, Ariel and Hannah, would work as assistants in this office. Their duties were to see to it that no one's rights were abrogated, and that the law of love was kept in letter and in spirit. They would also have oversight of all other offices. Everyone was of similar mind, so that was easy to do. The only records were the land grants given to every human being and the precise land surface that each entailed. They had this in electronic memory and also on a recorded deed. There was little need for this, because all land grants were forever, so there were no changes to record. That was a static part of the government because there was no more death or changes that death would make.

The ecology and environment were the most active areas of administration because a constant watch was kept to make sure that everything was in perfect balance. Nothing was allowed to hurt or destroy, but imbalances over time could occur which required vigilance and corrections. Many scientists were engaged all over the world taking readings and analyzing the physical conditions of the earth.

No one was better suited for this job than the Obadiahs. Benjamin and Deborah, as horticulturists of great distinction, seemed perfect to head this department. So with the Ancients' blessing Lev assigned them to it. They loved the plants and animals of the world, and they were unwilling that any should suffer by poor management. Rebekah, their daughter would also work with them as well as a staff of others.

Subduing the Earth

Man was to "replenish the earth, and subdue it" (Genesis 1:28). "Subduing" the earth was still the greatest challenge. For instance, most of the rivers in Russia flowed northward; whereas, if they flowed southward they would bring the fresh water to where the people were congregated. This way the rivers remained frozen most of the year and then yielded water to the North Pole. They had wanted to change the flow for a long time, but it seemed an impossible task…and then this needed to be analyzed to be sure they were not making a mistake.

Earthquakes, hurricanes, tornados and twisters had already been largely "subdued" but still work remained to calm the earth and make it friendlier. The world was full of scientists now and government was needed to have them working in unison on the problems. This department was expanding and needed to be coordinated for maximum effectiveness. This was Jake's area and he stepped into this office as the efficient and brilliant scientist that he was. He would surely not leave a stone unturned in arriving at a solution. Jake would be at home working with the world's scientists.

The world needed to maintain roads and bridges. With the increase in air travel, the great interstate highways needed removing to help the environment return to normal. In this regard some nations that were less advanced to start with were spared this task, because they planned for more air travel to avoid building highways that needed endless repair. Also, they had to make decisions about old historic sites that were in continuing disrepair. All buildings were in process of disintegration as the elements raged against them. Learning to build for eternity was the work of the future.

Annie (Jake's daughter) and her mother, Rachel, (Jake's former wife) were selected for this department along with Allon (Lev and Rebekah's son). They were pleased to be in this office with never-ending work. As people reported the need for work to be done, this department examined their plans and authorized the resources for them. As progress was made there would no longer be sand blowing in the wind or corrosive acids in the air. However, time would always assault what had been made, seeking to destroy it, even as the gentle rains wash away surfaces.

There were also many lesser functions that were orchestrated by the office of the Ancients and these, too, were filled with competent and loving people eager to serve God and their fellow men. There would be a seamless change of management, and the world would have a consistent and faithful rule of law.

By the end of the week everyone, under the loving direction of the Ancients, was at home with their workload. Government would continue, as it always had, with perfect people at the helm earnestly steering the ship of state.

The Ancients Are Taken

At the end of the week the Ancients submitted, for the first time, to a historical session where each was interviewed and photographed for the Hall of Fame Records. Each Ancient told the story of his or her previous life and the new life since being raised from the dead. It was thrilling to collect their personal testimonies of their former life, and that which they lived while serving the King. They also shared their joy as they anticipated a heavenly life. What a thrill to be standing at the threshold of a new heavenly home of which they knew nothing, except that they would see the face of God and of Christ! That was enough to satisfy the longings of their hearts.

On the final day, the Ancients all walked out of the city taking nothing with them. As they neared the old city of Bethany, they paused for prayer and a few hugs and farewells, and then they rose from the earth into a cloud and disappeared, just as Jesus had done at his ascension from the Mt. of Olives. A silence came over the earth and tears filled every eye.

Lev stood with his arms around Rebekah as they both tried to dry their eyes. The whole world was watching and fully aware of the intense drama. Never was everyone awake and looking on, as before their eyes some of the greatest people on earth were taken to heaven.

Lev closed his eyes in silent prayer. He thought of the great joy in heaven as God and Christ and his body members all received this loyal company into the heavenly courts. They had served God faithfully in two different worlds, and now they were raised to serve Him. How great was the rejoicing in heaven as the Father embraced His faithful servants, while bidding them enter the joys of their Lord!

Entering as Citizens of the New Jerusalem
(Book of Revelation)

21:22   And I saw no temple therein: for the Lord God Almighty and the Lamb are the temple of it.

21:23   And the city had no need of the sun, neither of the moon, to shine in it: for the glory of God did lighten it, and the Lamb [is] the light thereof.

21:24   And the nations of them which are saved shall walk in the light of it: and the kings [all people will be royalty — sons of God at this point] of the earth do bring their glory and honour into it.

21:25   And the gates of it shall not be shut at all by day: for there shall be no night there.

21:26   And they shall bring the glory and honour of the nations into it.

21:27   And there shall in no wise enter into it any thing that defileth, neither [whatsoever] worketh abomination, or [maketh] a lie: but they which are written in the Lamb's book of life.

22:1   And he showed me a pure river of water of life, clear as crystal, proceeding out of the throne of God and of the Lamb.

22:2   In the midst of the street of it, and on either side of the river, [was there] the tree of life, which bare twelve [manner of] fruits, [and] yielded her fruit every month: and the leaves of the tree [were] for the healing of the nations.

22:3   And there shall be no more curse: but the throne of God and of the Lamb shall be in it; and his servants shall serve him:

22:4   And they shall see his face; and his name [shall be] in their foreheads.

22:5 And there shall be no night there; and they need no candle, neither light of the sun; for the Lord God giveth them light: and they shall reign for ever and ever.

22:6 And he said unto me, These sayings [are] faithful and true: and the Lord God of the holy prophets sent his angel to show unto his servants the things which must shortly be done.

22:7 Behold, I come quickly: blessed [is] he that keepeth the sayings of the prophecy of this book.

22:14 Blessed [are] they that do his commandments, that they may have right to the tree of life, and may enter in through the gates into the city.

22:15 For without [are] dogs, and sorcerers, and whoremongers, and murderers, and idolaters, and whosoever loveth and maketh a lie.

22:16 I Jesus have sent mine angel to testify unto you these things in the churches. I am the root and the offspring of David, [and] the bright and morning star.

22:17 And the Spirit and the bride say, Come. And let him that heareth say, Come. And let him that is athirst come. And whosoever will, let him take the water of life freely.

THE END